THOSE KIDS FROM FAWN CREEK

FAWN CREEK K-12

SEVENTH GRADE

Max Bordelon

Greyson Broussard

Michael Colt

Abigail Crawford

Jane Crawford

Dorothy Doucet

Daelyn Guidry

Barnet Kingery

Lehigh Kingery

Daniel Landry

Hallie Romero

Baylee Trahan

Mr. Agosto

* Not Pictured:
Orchid Mason

i hate school -bArn

See you next year! -Baylee

ERIN ENTRADA KELLY

DAELYN

Lehigh

THOSE KIDS FROM FAWN CREEK

Luv u ♡ -hallie

Stay cool! -Daniel ☺

Greyson

Janie ♡

Didi ✳

that's me

Colt

have a great summer ☼ -Abby

just be you. -Orchid

MAX
(football 4ever!)

GREENWILLOW BOOKS
An Imprint of HarperCollinsPublishers

The author would like to acknowledge Sharon Huss Roat, Daniel Eaker, Lauren Liang, and the teams at HarperCollins/Greenwillow and Pippin Properties.

Those Kids from Fawn Creek
Copyright © 2022 by Erin Entrada Kelly
Interior illustrations by Celia Krampien

The text of this book is set in Source Serif Variable.
Book design by Sylvie Le Floc'h

Library of Congress Cataloging-in-Publication Data is available.
ISBN 978-0-06-297035-0 (hardback)
ISBN 978-0-06-297037-4 (ebook)
ISBN 978-0-06-324191-6 (international pbk ed.)

22 23 24 25 26 PC/LSCH 10 9 8 7 6 5 4 3 2 1
First Edition

 Greenwillow Books

To anyone with dreams
bigger than their hometowns

"Be nice. The world is a small town."
—Austin Kleon

WEEK ONE

1

On the day Orchid Mason walked through the door of Fawn Creek K–12, Greyson Broussard's right shoulder ached. A bruise would form there, he could tell.

Stupid Trevor.

Trevor had said he was "just kidding around" when he pinched and twisted Greyson's skin, but what kind of kidding is it when one person is laughing and the other wants to crawl into a hole and die? And he'd done it on the way to school, in the truck, with their dad *right there*, not saying or doing anything. As usual.

All because Greyson said he didn't want to go duck hunting.

"People'll start thinking you're soft, the way you go

around," his father had said, his meaty hand propped on the steering wheel as the truck pulled into the drop-off line. "Last I checked, I have two sons, not a son and a daughter."

That's when Trevor howled with laughter, even though it was an old joke, one their father had told many times before.

"He's already soft," Trevor said.

And that's when he'd pinched him.

Weren't older brothers supposed to be role models or something?

When the truck pulled into the circle, Greyson got out and lingered behind, like usual, watching his stupid brother take the front steps two at a time. It was Friday, November first, and Greyson was going to school, just like he'd done every week since the beginning of time, to see the same eleven classmates he'd known since the dawn of man, because in Fawn Creek the air was hot and humid, the mosquitoes nipped your arms, and nothing ever changed.

At that moment Greyson decided to let his mind float away from school, to the nearby creek. He imagined he was standing toe to water with a fishing rod in his hand. *The creek is quiet and there's no one around but me, the water, and the fish. No father. No brother. No school. Just me.*

He would have floated through the entirety of the morning if Dorothy hadn't kicked his chair and jolted him back to reality at the beginning of first period English. She did it lightly (Dorothy did everything lightly), but it was enough.

That's when he looked up.

The pain faded as soon as he saw her.

Not really, of course. But it seemed like it. The pinch disappeared; the hurt evaporated.

Mr. Agosto tapped his desk with his knuckles, even though everyone was already looking at him. Or, more accurately, looking at the girl standing by his side.

"Attention, all," Mr. Agosto said, his eyes shining. "We have a new student." It was obvious that Mr. Agosto was trying not to show his excitement. He made the same face when he introduced projects that he thought his students would be into, like writing imaginary letters to dead poets that none of them cared about. *Dear Emily Dickinson, Is it true that you wore a white dress and never left your house, or is that made up?* Greyson's letter had said. Even though Greyson didn't care much about Emily Dickinson's poetry, he'd been fascinated by the poet herself. She seemed so . . . mysterious.

And now he was fascinated by a new mystery—this girl, standing at the head of the class in a white T-shirt and breezy pleated skirt. Greyson's mother was a seamstress— she fixed hems, made decorative pillows, took in pageant and prom dresses—and he knew a pleated skirt when he saw one. The girl's hair was long. *Very* long. Past her waist. And wavy. No, not wavy. *Curly.* Big. Disheveled, but somehow looking like it was supposed to be that way. There was a white flower tucked behind her ear, even though it was November and no one was thinking about flowers. And who tucked flowers behind their ears, anyway?

Usually the twelve seventh graders were careful to leave their faces blank and expressionless. No one wanted to be the first to admit they were excited about anything. But this—a real-life new student, a real-life new *anything*—was far more interesting than any science experiment. People from Somewhere Else just didn't come to Fawn Creek. Certainly not unannounced. The next closest thing was Mr. Agosto, who was born in Venezuela and was the only non-white face in almost every room. But he had moved to Fawn Creek when he was three years old, because his dad got a job at Gimmerton, and—like Greyson, Dorothy, and virtually everyone else—he had never traveled outside of south Louisiana since then. The farthest he'd gone was Baton Rouge to go to Louisiana State, and that was just two hours away. *Small towns are like magnets,* Greyson's mother once said. *They pull you in and don't let go.*

And now the magnet had lured in a stranger. Janie and

Abby Crawford sat up straight and fixed their blue eyes on her. Greyson wondered what they were thinking. Max Bordelon, Daniel Landry, and Michael Colt, all of whom played youth football together in the next town, exchanged looks and smirks. Barnet and Lehigh Kingery slouched at their desks. The others shifted in their seats.

Greyson watched as the girl waved hello, like a royal greeting her subjects. The bangles on her wrist jangled. She smiled. A big, natural, easy smile that showed all her perfectly straight teeth. Daelyn Guidry and Baylee Trahan, who sat in the row next to him, pursed their lips. They'd both recently gotten braces. Hallie Romero—the third girl in their trio—had spent days trying to convince them they looked great.

Mr. Agosto continued, "Her name is—"

"I'm Orchid Mason," the girl said. She pointed to the only empty desk in the classroom. It was right next to Janie and Abby Crawford. "I'll just sit here, if that's okay."

She breezed to her new desk and sat down in one fluid movement.

She smelled like citrus.

And just like that, there were thirteen of them.

❀ 2 ❀

Before Orchid appeared, Mr. Agosto was teaching them the difference between a simile and a metaphor. A simile used the words "like" or "as." A metaphor didn't.

Dorothy Doucet sat at the back of the classroom. Dorothy Doucet always sat in the furthest back chair, as if she wanted to disappear into the wall. She looked like she wasn't paying attention. Her brown hair shielded her face. But this was an optical illusion, because Dorothy Doucet always paid attention.

Her eyes moved around the room, covertly assessing her classmates as she created her own metaphors and similes. She liked the idea that things didn't have to be exactly as they presented themselves.

Her best friend, Greyson, sat in front of her. She studied his shaggy blond hair and thought: *Greyson is like a yellow rose. But not a fresh one. More like pressed petals. The kind my mother puts between the pages of her Bible.*

Abby and Janie Crawford are poison ivy. They look safe, but they're dangerous in certain environments. Sometimes you don't know until it's too late.

Barnet and Lehigh Kingery are plants that don't need water. Leave them alone and they'll do their own thing, like my mother's succulents. Hardy and content to be solitary.

The demanding plants, the kind that don't have flowers, that's Max, Daniel, and Colt. They need lots of water and attention. They think they can grow on their own, but they can't.

Daelyn, Hallie, and Baylee are sweet-smelling daisies that lean toward the sun, wherever it leads them. They're bright and safe.

Just before Orchid walked in, Dorothy was trying to come up with a metaphor for herself.

I think I'm the dirt, she thought.

Then Orchid appeared.

In a small town like Fawn Creek—known as "Yawn Creek" by most of them—you'd think they would have known a new student was on her way. But Orchid caught them all off guard. Mr. Agosto was the only one who wasn't completely perplexed. When she knocked on the door, he waved her in and said, "Join us, join us!" like they were in the midst of a grand adventure and not enduring a language arts lesson.

When Orchid Mason walked into the classroom, Dorothy thought: *She is the girl in the fairy tale who drifts through a meadow and finds a prince.*

Or a spindle.

❀ *3* ❀

It would have been impossible for Mr. Agosto to continue droning on about metaphors and similes after Orchid's arrival. This particular group of Fawn Creek seventh graders had never seen a new student. If anything, just the opposite. Each year at least one of them left because a parent got a job somewhere else. Usually in Grand Saintlodge, which was the next town over. That's why there was one empty desk. It once belonged to Renni Dean.

The day had irreversibly tilted on its axis. Fridays were already disengaging, even without a new student, but now there was no hope of capturing anyone's attention. Mr. Agosto focused the spotlight on Orchid, which is where it shone anyway.

Greyson watched from his desk like everyone else, but his mind raced with a million questions. Where did this girl come from? Why was she wearing a flower in her hair? Why on earth was she at *this* school?

He fought the urge to turn around and talk to Dorothy. Together they could come up with a million questions and just as many answers. But that would have to wait until lunch.

Luckily, Mr. Agosto anticipated some of his curiosity.

"Orchid," Mr. Agosto said. "I have to admit, we don't get many new students at Fawn Creek. This is quite an event for us."

Janie and Abby Crawford rolled their eyes.

"Tell us, where did you move here from?" Mr. Agosto asked.

"Paris," Orchid replied.

Paris. One word. Just like that. *Paris.* As if she were naming some town down the road.

Greyson glanced at Janie and Abby. Abby sat up straight, like someone had poked her in the back with a pin. Janie's expression didn't change.

"Paris!" Mr. Agosto said. "How wonderful!"

Barnet Kingery leaned toward Daniel Landry. His desk squeaked against the floor. "Seriously?"

"No way," said Daniel.

Greyson's heart raced.

"Are you French or something?" Baylee asked.

Greyson had noticed that Baylee started wearing makeup this year. She didn't quite know how to wear it, though. The lines around her eyes were crooked, and the blush on her cheeks was a bit too pink. Not that Greyson knew how to wear makeup. He just noticed things like that, even if he never commented on them. Except to Dorothy, sometimes.

Orchid laughed. An airy laugh, not a mocking one.

"Me? Oh no, I'm not French. I was born in New York," she said.

"New York *City*?" asked Hallie Romero.

Hallie traded looks with Daelyn and Baylee, whose new braces now seemed like boring old news, even though they had dominated their conversations all last week. One of them would ask, "Are you sure I look okay?" and the other would say "Of course, you look amazing," back and forth, back and forth, like a tennis match of reassurances. Greyson had listened from his desk. He'd thought about saying, "You look great, don't worry about it," or "They'll be off before you know it," but he didn't open his mouth. He wasn't sure if they'd be grateful or weirded out, and even though he had known them his whole life—he knew, for example, that the tiny scar on Daelyn's chin was from when she fell off the monkey bars in second grade, and that Baylee's godfather died two years ago from Alzheimer's—he wasn't about to take his chances.

"Yep, New York City," Orchid said. "The one and only."

Mr. Agosto cleared his throat. His eyes darted around the room like he was nervous that the day would run away from him and he'd never catch it again.

"Well, well," he said. "I knew we had a new student arriving today, but I didn't realize she'd be so well traveled."

Greyson imagined Orchid on the streets of New York City, buying hot dogs from a street vendor or hurrying toward the subway. Then he pictured her sitting on an airplane, looking out the window. She seemed like the type who would choose the window seat. *I know I will, if I ever get the chance to fly,* Greyson thought. She probably had a passport tucked away in a drawer somewhere with a dozen stamps in it. It wasn't hard to imagine any of these things. But when he tried to place her here, in Fawn Creek, Louisiana—a town that didn't have a single stoplight—it was difficult to believe.

Yet here she was.

4

Janie Crawford thought: *Big deal.*

She thought: *What's in Paris, anyway? The Eiffel Tower? Woo-woo. And who cares if she's from New York City? Everyone knows the people in New York are rude and aggressive and crowd all the sidewalks. Who wants to live in a place where you can't even breathe? People think New York is all that just because it's in movies and TV shows.*

Okay, so maybe Janie didn't have firsthand experience with New York City, but whatever. She didn't care about New York or Paris, and she certainly didn't care about this new girl, with her wild hair and that stupid flower behind her ear like she's . . . like she's . . . like she's what?

"A fairy princess," Janie mumbled.

Her cousin Abby turned around.

"Did you say something?" Abby said.

"Hm?" Janie made a point to look bored. Not just by Abby's question, but by everything. If people wanted to get all gaga and uncivilized over some new girl, let them. The way their faces were all lit up, you'd think they'd never seen a new person ever in their entire lives. The self-proclaimed "God Squad"—Daelyn, Baylee, and Hallie—looked at Orchid like she was the queen of England or whatever. And the boys! Like dumb, drooling puppies. She noticed Michael Colt's eyes swing again and again in Orchid's direction, even though he was trying to be cool about it.

Wait until I tell Renni, Janie thought. Renni and Colt had broken up a while ago, but still.

And Max had looked at Orchid, too, hadn't he?

Janie shifted in her seat. Oh, who cared about Max Bordelon, anyway?

"I thought you said something," Abby whispered.

Mr. Agosto was writing some nonsense on the whiteboard, with his back facing them.

"I didn't say a word," Janie replied.

Abby nodded discreetly toward Orchid, whose eyes were looking straight ahead. A single notebook was on her desk and she had her hands folded on top of it like she was *so* prim and proper. Whatever.

"We should ask her to sit with us at lunch," Abby said.

"Absolutely not," said Janie.

"Why not?"

"So we can watch Barn and Slowly act like idiots? No thank you." It was bad enough that they had to sit with Barnet and Lehigh, who everyone called "Slowly," in the first place. No girl in their right mind would willingly sit with the Kingery boys, but they were Janie's cousins, so it couldn't be helped. Being nice was such a *pain* sometimes.

"Who cares? They act like idiots anyway."

Janie leaned forward and locked eyes with her cousin. God, Abby could be so naive. Sometimes Janie didn't know who was worse—Abby, who had the brain of an eight-year-old, or Janie's bratty little sister Madeline, who was an actual eight-year-old.

"I don't want a fifth person at our table," Janie said, pressing her fingertip against the desk for emphasis.

Abby raised her hands in mock defeat. "Okay, okay. Geez." She turned back around.

Janie smiled to herself. No, they did *not* need a fifth person, thank you very much. For the past two years, it had been just the four of them: her, Abby, Barn, and Slowly. And even though Barn and Slowly "weren't the brightest bulbs in the box," as Janie's father would say, the four of them had reputations as far as Fawn Creek was concerned.

They were like Fawn Creek royalty. The Crawfords—Janie and Abby's family—owned the restaurant and grocery in town, and the Kingerys—Barn and Slowly's family—had the bait and tackle shop. Their family names were on signs all over.

"People look up to us in this town, Janie," her mother often said. "You gotta be careful who you go around with. When people talk about you, it reflects a certain way on me and your daddy."

And who knew about this Orchid girl? Janie had never even heard of her before she showed up. No murmurings at lunch or on the walk home from school. She just arrived. *Poof. Here I am, long-lost daughter of Paris and New York, and I'm just going to sit right here in Renni Dean's old desk like I own the place.*

Janie understood, even if Abby didn't. They had to align themselves with the right people. Poor Abby was too naive to know the difference.

Luckily, Janie thought, *she has me.*

❀ 5 ❀

"We should invite her to sit with us," Greyson said.

Orchid walked through the lunchroom like a ghost. She moved slowly and dreamily, like a bird looking for a place to land. Her eyes—big and blue (or were they green?)—wandered over each table. Fawn Creek K–12 was a small school, to say the least. Thirty-nine middle schoolers in all, but they still managed to separate themselves into tightly knit groups.

Orchid studied each table but never stopped. She passed the seventh graders, the eighth graders, and then the pockets of students swallowed her up and Greyson lost sight of her.

"I can't see her anymore," Greyson said, craning his neck this way and that.

"Did you see how many apples she had on her tray?" Dorothy said, across from him. "How can one person like apples that much?"

Greyson sighed. "You should go find her and ask her to sit with us."

Dorothy's eyes widened as if Greyson had asked her to murder someone.

"Me? Why me?" she said.

"Because you're a girl."

"And? So what?"

"I can't walk up to some new girl and ask her to sit with me. She'll think I'm weird or some kind of creeper."

"What if she thinks *I'm* weird and a creeper?"

"It's not weird if a girl wants to be friends with another girl. But a guy just walking up to some random girl at lunch?" Greyson shook his head. "No."

"Excuse me," Dorothy said. "But you're a guy and I'm a girl and *we* have lunch every day."

"You know what I mean." Greyson popped a tater tot in his mouth. "What if she becomes friends with the Crawfords because she doesn't know any better?"

Dorothy glanced at the Crawford cousins.

"What would I even say?" Dorothy said, her voice low. A blush of red crawled up her neck. The "red dread," Dorothy called it. When she was nervous, the red dread clawed its way from her chest to the tips of her ears. It wasn't that bad at the moment, though. Not yet.

"Let's not worry about it now," Greyson said, making sure to focus on Dorothy's face. "We'll ask her together on Monday."

Dorothy paused. "What if . . . "

"What if what?"

"I don't know." Dorothy shrugged. Her skin was already reverting to its original color. "What if we don't like her? What if she doesn't fit in with us? I mean. Three's a crowd. Right?"

"Colt, Daniel, and Max hang out all the time and there's three of them."

"Yeah, but Max doesn't count. He only has half a brain," said Dorothy. "In first grade he used to eat mulch from the playground, remember?"

"What about Daelyn, Baylee, and Hallie?"

Dorothy paused. "They have God as part of their group. God counts as one. At least."

Greyson sighed. This conversation wouldn't go anywhere, and he knew it. Dorothy just didn't like change. Usually Greyson was okay with that. But this was different. This was a *new* girl. New kids never came to Fawn Creek, especially not with wild hair and flowers behind their ears.

He wanted to know what she was like.

He wanted to hear about Paris.

❀ 6 ❀

Dorothy felt like a piece of furniture at home. She felt like one of the side chairs with striped upholstery in the living room, something that her parents brought home one day but then didn't pay much attention to.

Her parents went through all the right motions. Especially Dorothy's mother. When Dorothy got home after school, she knew Mrs. Doucet would be in the kitchen, slicing an apple or peeling an orange for Dorothy's afternoon snack. She knew her mother would place the fruit on a plate. She knew her mother would set the plate on the table next to a folded paper towel. And she knew her mother would ask about her day.

How was your day? her mother would ask.

Fine, Dorothy would respond, and she would eat her snack dutifully, just as she had every day since first grade.

And then Dorothy would go to her room and she'd stay there until dinner, when her father would come home from his job at Gimmerton Chemical. They would eat at the table, but no one would really say anything. The clink of forks and spoons against plates would be the loudest sound in the room. They were in a play, and this was the scene where they ate dinner together as a family. Each of them had an assigned role. Hardworking father. Caring mother. Dutiful daughter.

But tonight, Dorothy actually had something to share. Some news.

"We got a new student at school today," she said, staring at her pot roast.

"Really?" Mrs. Doucet said, a lilt of surprise in her voice. And why wouldn't she be surprised? New students didn't just arrive at Fawn Creek, after all. "I didn't hear about anyone new moving to town."

Dorothy lifted her eyes and shrugged. Her father's mouth was full and round with food.

"Did anyone new start at the plant?" Mrs. Doucet asked her husband.

Dorothy's father swallowed and shook his head. "Not that I know of. I haven't seen anyone new on my shift, anyways."

Dorothy moved the cooked carrots around on her plate. She didn't really like pot roast, though she'd never said anything. Part of her role as dutiful daughter was to keep her opinions to herself. The striped side chair never complained, and she wouldn't, either.

"She's from New York City," she said.

"New York City!" exclaimed Mrs. Doucet. "How strange."

"I certainly haven't heard of anyone from New York City," Dorothy's father said. "I don't know what someone from New York would want with this place."

Dorothy looked at her parents. She wondered what they were thinking. Their faces were like stone—"faces like stone" was a simile, she noted to herself—and it was hard to determine what simmered underneath their exteriors, if anything. They were nothing like other parents. For one thing, they were older. They'd been married for a long time before Dorothy came along. Her mother was forty-five when she was born. Dorothy had been told many times that she was a "complete surprise."

Surprises weren't always good, were they?

Dorothy had a theory about her parents. Her theory was this: They never wanted to have children. But then it happened—surprise!—and they had no other choice but to play their roles to the best of their ability. Dorothy wasn't sure when she'd come to this conclusion. Maybe she was born knowing she was the third wheel, which was why she always did the best she could to be a good daughter. She never wanted them to whisper to each other at night, *See? This is why we never wanted kids in the first place!* If she made herself like the furniture, they'd never have a reason to be disappointed.

Dorothy had never shared this theory with anyone, not even Greyson. The closest she came was in a creative writing assignment they'd had last year. Mrs. Roat told them to write from the point of view of an inanimate object. Dorothy wrote about a rocking chair who desperately wanted to be part of the human family who owned her. When Greyson finished reading it, he didn't say anything for a long time. Then he told her it was the best story he'd ever read.

Then he'd said, "I wish I was a piece of furniture in my house."

"Why?" she'd asked.

"Because," he said. "Nobody talks to the furniture."

❀ 7 ❀

Greyson had two places of refuge at home, besides his bedroom. One of them was the small patio facing the fenced backyard, where the family's chocolate Lab, Zucchini, spent most of her time.

After school Greyson tossed his backpack aside and went straight for the sliding glass door. Trevor was making a sandwich in the kitchen and bouncing around to music from his earbuds. Greyson breezed by him without stopping.

Zucchini was already on the shaded patio. Her tail wagged wildly and she pattered her feet, trying really hard not to jump on him. She was well trained.

Greyson sat on the concrete instead of the patio furniture. Zucchini nearly knocked him over with affection.

"How was your day, Zuke?" asked Greyson. "Were you a good girl?"

The night they brought Zucchini home, she was small but had enormous paws. Greyson and Trevor were small, too—five and eight years old—but were already on their way to being enemies. They'd argued over what to name her as their mother finished making dinner. When Trevor saw the baked zucchini, he scrunched up his nose and complained. Greyson did, too. It was one of the few things they agreed on.

"We should name the dog Zucchini," their mother said. "So you can never say 'I hate zucchini' ever again."

And that was that.

Technically, Zucchini belonged to Greyson's father, Mr. Broussard. He bought and trained her for duck hunting. According to Mr. Broussard, Zuke was the best hunting dog he'd ever had, and he treated her as such. He bathed her when she got muddy. He took her with him on errands. He brought her to the vet to get her shots. Every night before he went to bed, Mr. Broussard carried a food bowl outside for Zuke and kissed her on the head before she started eating.

Greyson couldn't remember the last time his father had hugged him.

Zucchini settled down next to Greyson and laid her head in his lap. He felt the heft of her against him. He didn't mind. He took his phone out of his back pocket and searched for Orchid online while absently stroking the dog's ears.

He visited every social media platform but couldn't find a single profile that belonged to Orchid Mason. There wasn't much in general under that name. Just places.

The *Orchid Mason* neighborhood of Charlotte, North Carolina.

Orchid Mason Lane in Argyle, Texas.

Orchid Mason Apartments in Burlington, Vermont.

No *Orchid Mason*, twelve-year-old girl.

Well, that wasn't so strange, was it? Greyson didn't really use social media, either. Neither did Dorothy. And he was pretty sure he wasn't on the internet anywhere.

He googled himself, to be sure. To his surprise, there were several results. Not many, but a few. A comment he left on a YouTube video last year. Photos from the Fawn Creek K–12 website. There was a thread from "G Broussard" on a Kate Middleton fansite, which he'd forgotten about. His chest warmed with embarrassment. What if someone searched his name and found this?

He plucked Orchid out of his brain and did an image search for Kate Middleton, Duchess of Cambridge, instead. He glanced through the patio door as the photos loaded to make sure Trevor was nowhere around. Greyson spent an inordinate amount of time looking at images of Kate Middleton, especially when there was nothing else to do. It's not that he liked her or anything—not in *that* way. But she had recently worn a red coatdress with front-button detailing and a matching pillbox hat. It was the most beautiful thing Greyson had ever seen. He liked how she looked in that dress. She wore the dress and the dress wore her.

He thought about his own clothes. They were uninspiring, to say the least. And, despite the fact that it was November, they were now sticky from the heat and humidity.

Time to go inside.

He scratched Zuke behind the ears one last time then went in. But instead of going into his bedroom, he opted for his other refuge: his mom's sewing room. It was his favorite room of the house. The only bad thing was, it had a door that other people could open, like Trevor did now, less than five minutes after Greyson sat down on the floor.

"Hey, whatcha doing in there?" Trevor said, poking his head through the door. "Making pretty dresses?" He let out one loud laugh and disappeared.

Too bad it wasn't Tuesday or Thursday. Those were the afternoons when Trevor had driver's ed. As soon as Trevor turned fifteen, he begged his parents to enroll him. He was signed up less than two weeks later. What Trevor wanted, he got.

Greyson couldn't wait for the day Trevor got his license. Maybe he'd drive away and never come back.

Besides, Greyson wasn't making pretty dresses. He wasn't making anything. He was just sitting on the floor, surrounded by pillows, pants, and skirts, scrolling on his phone. His screen was tipped upward, protected from prying eyes. Trevor had a habit of making fun of whatever Greyson was looking at, so he'd learned to keep his screen out of view any time he was home, even if no one was around.

He closed his tabs and thought about calling Dorothy, but her father didn't like it when she spent too much time on her phone.

He leaned his head against a row of pillows. He heard the front door open. Mom was home.

Stupid Trevor. No one *made* dresses in here. Not even their mother. She mostly adjusted hemlines and made custom pillowcases with inspirational quotes stitched on them. She got most of her business through Facebook, where she'd post pictures and ask for orders. Pillowcases were draped all around the room with half-stitched quotes like *Live, Laugh, Love* or *Dance Like Nobody's Watching*. It was getting close to Christmas, which meant the room would be piled high with them soon enough. The people of Fawn Creek, Louisiana, loved to be inspired by their housewares, and his mother was happy to oblige.

Speaking of which.

"Hi, sunbeam," she said. "I thought I'd find you in here."

His mother came in wearing jeans and an LSU T-shirt. Everyone in Fawn Creek followed LSU football like it was their religion. Very few people in town went to LSU— or any college, for that matter—and Baton Rouge was a couple of hours away, but Louisiana pride wasn't limited by alma maters or geography. Greyson didn't mind watching football. It was one of the few activities that he shared with his father and brother. They would gather in the living room, surrounded by nachos and pizza and hot wings, and watch the Tigers trounce their opponents. Greyson cheered when they cheered and cursed when they cursed, but there were times when he secretly rooted for the other team. LSU was a football powerhouse—they won game after game. A sports announcer once said that LSU had one of the loudest football stadiums in the country because there were so many fans. *Just once,* Greyson would think, *it would be nice if an underdog came along and surprised everyone.*

"What're you up to in here?" his mom asked. "Talking to Dorothy?"

"No," Greyson said. "Just scrolling."

She leaned against the doorframe. "How was your day?"

Greyson shrugged. "We got a new student."

"Really? I didn't hear about anyone moving to town."

"Her name is Orchid."

"What's her last name?"

"Mason, I think."

Mrs. Broussard narrowed her eyes and stared at the air, thinking. "That's strange. I definitely don't know anyone named Mason," she said. It was strange indeed. It was nearly impossible to move to a town like Fawn Creek without someone knowing about it. "What does she look like?"

"She's got long, long hair. It's kinda wild looking, but pretty. And she had a flower in her hair, which was kinda random, but it worked. And she loves apples."

Mrs. Broussard raised her eyebrows. "Sounds like you might have a crush."

Greyson sighed. Pulled out his phone again.

"You're the one who asked what she looked like," he mumbled.

His mother winked, then left the room.

❀ 8 ❀

Janie Crawford wasn't exactly in love with the idea of smelling like seafood all the time, but it was a small price to pay when your family owned the most successful restaurant in town.

Okay, the only restaurant in town.

Still. It was successful, and everyone knew about it, which meant everyone knew the Crawfords, and Janie was a Crawford, so there you go.

Crawford's Restaurant wasn't fancy by any standard, but you couldn't live in Fawn Creek without eating there at least a few times a year, and not just because there was no other choice. Crawford's had the best shrimp and crawfish étouffée, the best pistolettes, the best crab legs, the best everything. People from Saintlodge drove forty-five minutes out of their way to get lunch there on Saturdays, which was exactly why Renni Dean sauntered in with her parents on this particular Saturday.

Janie was sort of working, which meant she was half-heartedly wiping down tables while inwardly complaining that neither of her parents was paying for her services and that her sister Madeline was not subjected to such servitude, never mind that Mee-Wee was only eight.

In the midst of all this mental bellyaching, Renni came up behind her and poked her in the back. It startled Janie enough that she dropped the rag and whipped around, ready to pounce, but when she realized it was Renni, she relaxed and said, "Why didn't you text me back, loser?"

"I was about to, but then I told my parents to just drive me here. I get *so bored* in that big, drafty house. I thought, *Why not go see Janie and hear this hot news she has to tell me?*"

Renni sat down at the table Janie had been cleaning. Her parents were at the counter, talking to Janie's aunt, who worked every Saturday. Janie's aunt was named Kimberly, but everyone called her Kiki, who knows why, and Janie was certain without being able to hear their conversation that Kiki was asking Renni's father if there were any openings at the refinery in Saintlodge, since Mr. Dean was now a manager, which is why Renni had a "big, drafty house," which she always mentioned, as if Janie didn't know Renni's house was now bigger than the Crawford house—whatever.

"So?" said Renni. She twisted a lock of shiny brown hair around her finger. "What was your mysterious text about?"

Janie sat down, too, even though she wasn't supposed to. Technically, she was working.

"This new girl showed up at Fawn Creek yesterday," Janie said.

Renni leaned back. "A new girl at Fawn Creek? What, is she being punished for something?"

Renni laughed lightly and Janie did, too, even though she really didn't think it was funny how Renni thought she was suddenly better than everyone just because she moved to Grand Saintlodge, like Saintlodge was some kind of metropolis. It's not like it was *New York* or something, geez.

Speaking of which.

"Yeah, well, she might be trapped here, but from what I could tell, *certain people* didn't seem to mind," said Janie.

Renni leaned forward and narrowed her eyes. Renni had recently started wearing light blue eyeliner because she said blue eyeliner went better with brown eyes, and maybe she was right, but Janie thought it looked kind of silly, the way Renni tried to curl up the liner at the ends.

"Like who?" Renni asked. "Barn and Slowly?" She pretended to gag.

"Colt," Janie replied, triumphantly. "He was staring at her like he had no sense."

That was something Janie's mother always said. *That man is staring at me like he has no sense.*

Renni straightened up then and said, "Describe her to me."

Janie *hated* when Renni used that tone. *Describe her to me.* Like Janie was her servant and was expected to follow commands. But maybe that wasn't too far off, because Janie always obliged. Like right now.

"She's got long, brown hair. Super curly and kinda"— Janie waved her hands around her head, mimicking Orchid's hair—"wild."

"What do you mean, 'wild'?"

"Hm. Kinda like that red-haired girl in that Disney movie we watched in the theater room last year," Janie said, both as a reference for Renni and as a way to remind her that the Crawfords had a spare room in their house that was just for watching movies. Janie's dad had set it up with an oversized sofa and giant TV and everything. He'd put blackout blinds on the windows so the room would be pitch-black and a refrigerator in the corner for soda and snacks. *You're not the only one with a big house,* Janie thought.

Renni huffed. "That girl wasn't even pretty."

"Well, she doesn't look like that girl. Just her hair. Kind of." Janie paused. "And she had a flower in it."

Renni raised an eyebrow. "A flower? In her hair?"

"Yep."

"What, does she think she's some kinda hippie or something?"

"She's from New York."

Now both of Renni's eyebrows went up. "New York? And she moved *here?*"

"She lived in New York *and* Paris."

"Come on."

"I'm serious."

Renni pulled out her phone. "Give me her name."

"You won't find her online anywhere," Janie said. At the counter, Kiki gave her a look that said *If you have time to lean, you have time to clean.* Janie grabbed the rag and stood up. "I already tried."

"Tell me anyway."

There she went again with the demands.

Renni was so irritating sometimes.

But, once again, Janie followed orders.

"Orchid Mason," Janie said.

9

There weren't many perfect-weather days in Fawn Creek. The summers were brutally hot and humid, and they lasted forever. When the cold months came—and there weren't many—it was just enough to nip the air and send you indoors.

Before Orchid showed up, the air was heavy and stifling. But the week after she appeared, it changed. When Monday rolled around, it was seventy degrees with low humidity.

Maybe that's why Greyson was in a good mood.

Maybe that's why he suggested, insisted, and ultimately volunteered to invite Orchid to their lunch table.

"Come on, let's find her," he said. He stood, walked

around the table—the same table where he'd sat across from Dorothy for the past seven years—and pulled at Dorothy's shirtsleeve until she got up.

Dorothy walked beside him with her head down and arms folded. She looked like a wilted flower as they crossed the cafeteria. The Crawfords and the Kingerys eyed them.

They found Orchid. She wasn't at a table. She was leaning against the wall in the corner, near the window, eating an apple, with a faraway look in her eyes. Her hair was pulled up in a huge, beautiful, messy bun that sat atop her head. No flower. She was wearing a white boatneck shirt with a small rip in the collar.

"Hi," Greyson said. He imagined stitching the collar for her.

Orchid didn't react at first, and for a moment Greyson had the ridiculous thought that she was a hallucination. The way the sunlight touched her face. The small, delicate bite in the apple. The strange glow in her eyes.

"Hi," he said again, a bit louder.

She blinked and turned away from the window, which opened toward a small overgrown field and an old, unused basketball court.

"Hi," said Orchid. She smiled.

Greyson could have sworn that her eyes twinkled.

"Hi," said Greyson, for what he now realized was the

third time in a row. He cleared his throat. "We were just wondering"—he motioned toward Dorothy, who still had her head down—"if you wanted to sit at our table."

"Your table?" Orchid repeated, as if he was speaking a language she didn't understand. Her eyes flitted to Dorothy, then back to him. "Actually, I was going to ask if you two wanted to sit with *me*." She raised a slender finger to the window and whispered, "Outside."

"Outside?" said Greyson.

"We certainly like to repeat each other, don't we?" Orchid said. She giggled.

Greyson's heart thundered in his chest. *Thwap-Thwap-Thwap.*

"No one sits out there," Greyson said.

Orchid looked at Dorothy. Back at Greyson.

"Why not?" she asked.

"Because . . . " Greyson's sentence drifted away. He couldn't remember why, exactly.

Orchid raised her eyebrows. Greyson noticed a small leaf in her hair, trapped in that chaotic bun. The sounds of the cafeteria bounced off the walls around them. Kids laughing and hollering. Chairs moving. Trays rattling.

"It's a beautiful day," Orchid said. "When you get a beautiful day, you have to catch it. Like a firefly."

"You sound like one of my mother's pillowcases,"

Greyson said. Immediately his entire body burned with embarrassment. *You sound like one of my mother's pillowcases?* Why did he have to say something so stupid?

But Orchid simply took a bite of her apple. She chewed and chewed. Swallowed.

"Your mother's pillowcases are very wise," she said, as a line of juice snaked down her chin.

$\circledast\,10\,\circledast$

Dorothy didn't want to go outside. Dorothy was perfectly content to stay at the same table for the rest of the year, and the year after that and the year after that. Dorothy may have only had one friend, but she didn't need more. Dorothy did not want to talk to a stranger. Besides, something about Orchid made her feel small. Like she was shrinking. It wasn't anything the new girl did, necessarily. It was just her presence. Orchid wasn't a thunderstorm or a virus, like Renni Dean. She was more like . . .

Hm.

More like what?

Dorothy bit her bottom lip, trying to think of a good simile as she followed Greyson and Orchid to the shadowy hall at the back of the cafeteria. They walked stealthily, as if they were doing something wrong. Were they? It was hard to tell. Dorothy couldn't remember anyone saying they were *forbidden* to go outside.

The door to the outside was at the end of the hallway, which was lined with stacks of boxes. Cafeteria supplies, from the looks of the labels: Dispenser Napkins and Salt Packets and Plastic Straws.

"The door might be locked," Greyson whispered to Orchid.

"There's only one way to find out," Orchid replied. She glanced over her shoulder then maneuvered around the boxes, leading the way.

Dorothy didn't have to look to know people were watching.

You couldn't do anything in Fawn Creek without people watching.

She felt the eyes of Janie and Abby Crawford burn through her back, which meant that the Kingery boys—Barn and Slowly—were watching, too. Dorothy didn't really care what the Kingerys thought—who did?—but the Crawfords gave her the red dread, even though she had once spent the night at Abby Crawford's house for Abby's seventh birthday and remembered the time in third grade when Janie cried because a ribbon had fallen out of her hair, lost forever, until Dorothy found it under a chair. But that was before they had all fractioned themselves into little groups.

Dorothy held her breath when Orchid leaned on the push bar of the door. What if an alarm went off? She glanced back quickly, ready to bolt, but there was no sound. Only sunlight flooding the hallway.

"Come on," Orchid chirped as she ran toward the grass.

Greyson and Dorothy followed.

❀ *11* ❀

Janie sat at the red table near the corner, like always, with Abby on one side of her and their cousins, Barn and Slowly, sitting across from them. Being around the Kingery boys felt more like babysitting than socializing, but here they were, year after year, sitting together because they were family and "there's nothing more important than family," at least according to Janie's mother.

Janie and Abby watched Orchid, Greyson, and Dorothy sneak out the back door.

"What are they even *doing*?" Janie said.

"They went outside," Slowly replied.

Janie rolled her eyes.

Well, duh.

See, this was why Slowly didn't have much "social stock," as Janie's mother would say. You'd think the Kingery boys would be popular just because of who they were—the Kingerys had their names on just as many business signs as the Crawfords—but it hadn't worked out that way for them. Unlike Janie and Abby, who were considered by many (including themselves) to be *the* prettiest and *the* most popular girls in grades six through eight, Barnet and Lehigh Kingery lingered somewhere on the pitiful end of the social pool. They were saved only by their family name. But they weren't unscathed. Take Lehigh, for instance. He'd been called Lee as a kid, but then he started Fawn Creek Elementary and it became clear that he couldn't keep up with the rest of the class. That's when someone—Renni, probably—named him "Slow Lee." She'd even made a chant out of it, according to Fawn Creek legend. Soon he was "Slowly" to everyone and no one really remembered when or how it started, only that it was.

Janie and Abby often wondered (behind the boys' backs, of course) if Barn or Slowly would ever find girlfriends and get married. Who would want to be with them?

Dorothy Doucet, maybe. She'd probably be grateful for any form of attention. Which is why it figured—*just figured*—that she'd attached herself to the new girl. She was so hungry for a friend that she came out of her shell to latch onto Orchid Whatshername.

Pathetic.

"If Mr. Shaughnessy finds out they went out there, they're gonna be in trouble," Barn said, his mouth full. "Everyone knows we don't go out there."

Abby cocked her head and said, "Yeah, but why?"

"Why what?" Barn asked.

"Why don't we ever go out there?"

A moment's silence lingered over them.

"Because," Janie finally said. She sipped from her reusable water bottle, the pink one with the white polka dots that cost forty dollars and her father said, "Forty dollars for a water bottle? Seriously?" but it was only because he "didn't know the finer things in life," according to Janie's mother, who was often right.

"Because why?" Abby said.

Janie sighed. "Because it's a billion degrees outside and they're going to be covered in mosquito bites from head to toe in about ten seconds. Watch. They'll probably need a blood transfusion."

"We should have asked her to sit with us, like I suggested," Abby said.

"Why would we do that?" Barn said. "She looks dirty. All that hair."

This was ironic since Barn's aversion to bathing was practically legendary, but no one pointed that out.

"Because she's new and needs to make friends with the right people," Abby said.

Janie shook her head. "No way. Our loyalty is to Renni."

"What does Renni have to do with anything? She doesn't even go here anymore."

Oh, Abby. Poor, naive Abby.

"Colt likes the new girl. And Renni is our friend," Janie said.

"I thought Colt and Renni broke up, like, two months ago," said Abby. "Besides, since when does Colt like Orchid?"

Janie didn't know if he liked her for certain, of course. It was just a hunch. But the best part of a hunch is when you discover that you're right.

"Since about two seconds after she walked in on Friday," Barn said. His fingertips were greasy and covered with salt. He licked them clean as he spoke. "He's gonna ask her to meet him at the football game on Saturday."

Abby's face lit up. She loved gossip more than anyone Janie knew. Except maybe for Janie herself.

"Really?" Abby said. "How do you know?"

"What do you mean, how do I know? I just know."

"Well, you have to know *somehow*."

"Colt told Max and Daniel, and we heard," Slowly said, his hands in his lap. He wasn't the finger-licking type. Thank God.

"So it's confirmed, then," Janie said, pulling out her phone and consciously not-reacting to the sound of Max Bordelon's name. "And I was right to not invite her to our table. When Renni finds out, she's going to *flip*."

She hadn't even finished her sentence before she started texting.

12

Dorothy swatted a mosquito that buzzed near her ear as she followed Orchid through the grass to the edge of the basketball court. When Orchid sat on the concrete beneath the rusted, netless rim of the basketball hoop, Dorothy and Greyson did, too. The grass was overgrown, partly obstructing their view of the lunchroom window. Dorothy was nervous, though she didn't know why. The red dread threatened to crawl up her neck, but as long as she stayed quiet, she could keep it at bay.

"Are you really from Paris?" Greyson asked.

"No, I'm from New York," said Orchid. She took a final bite of her apple, threw the core into the tall grass, and wiped her fingertips gently on the hem of her shirt.

"Oh, yeah, you said that. I forgot." Greyson raised his eyebrows. "So you were, like, born there?"

Dorothy suddenly thought of their lunch trays, still on the table, waiting for them to come back. She imagined she was there now and it was just any other Monday. She looked toward the window to see if there were faces pressed against the glass, watching them, but she couldn't tell. The windowpane reflected the sky and the grass was in the way.

"Yes, but I've moved around a lot," Orchid said.

"Is your dad in the military?" Greyson asked.

Orchid tilted her head, her mouth a tight line. "Why do you ask? Did you hear something?"

"Oh," he said. "No. I guess I just thought that . . . "

Orchid smiled and laughed lightly. Her bracelets jingled like wind chimes. It wasn't flirty, exactly, though Dorothy wasn't completely sure what real flirting looked like. It felt more like the gesture of an old friend. There was something familiar about the way Orchid was acting. Like she'd met them years ago and was thrilled to be reunited.

"Sorry to get so serious all of a sudden," Orchid said. She pursed her lips. "Let's just say that I've had to move a lot and I can't really talk about it." A mosquito hovered in front of her. She waved it away. Her movements were refined and delicate.

Dorothy's hands fidgeted in her lap.

"By the way, I have a super-important question to ask both of you," Orchid said. She fixed her eyes on Dorothy. Orchid's eyes were a strange color. Almost purple.

Orchid's eyes were like violets.

The red dread prickled under Dorothy's skin. What would she ask? What super-important question could this girl possibly have? And what if she, Dorothy, didn't know the answer?

Orchid raised her eyebrows, leaned forward, and said: "What are your names?"

Dorothy could practically feel Greyson exhale next to her.

"I'm Greyson," he said.

Dorothy hoped he would introduce her, too. *I'm Greyson, and this is my best friend, Dorothy.* Instead, both Greyson and Orchid looked at her and waited.

"Dorothy," said Dorothy.

"Greyson and Dorothy," repeated Orchid. She nodded, like she was doing calculations in her head. "How do you feel about that?"

"About what?" Greyson said.

"Your names."

A mosquito landed on Orchid's arm. She didn't swat it away.

"Oh." Greyson fidgeted. "I don't know. I never really thought about it."

"Really? You should! Your name is very important. You should spend *a lot* of time thinking about it."

Greyson shrugged. "It doesn't really matter. It's not like we're able to pick our own names. We're just kinda stuck with whatever our parents give us."

Orchid snapped her fingers and pointed at him. "That's exactly why you should spend a lot of time thinking about it." She looked at Dorothy. "What about you, Dorothy?"

Dorothy's heart whooshed in her ears. She had a lot to say on the matter, actually. She just couldn't gather the words.

"It's okay, I guess," Dorothy said finally. Her voice was quiet. Like a mouse.

"Just okay?" Orchid said. The mosquito on her arm flew away. Dorothy wondered if it would leave a welt. At the moment, though, Orchid's skin was smooth and flawless, as if she hadn't been bitten at all.

"I hate my name," Dorothy blurted. She hadn't planned on sharing that, but it spilled out anyway.

"Why?" Orchid asked.

Dorothy shrugged. "I just do."

"There are a lot of great Dorothys." Orchid counted on her fingers, naming a slew of Dorothys that Dorothy had never heard of. "Dorothy Parker. Dorothy Dandridge. Dorothy Gale. Dorothy Allison."

"What about Dorothy from *The Wizard of Oz*?" Greyson asked.

"That's Dorothy Gale," Orchid said.

Dorothy plucked a blade of grass that had pushed its way through the cement.

"I still hate it," Dorothy said.

"I understand. When you're given the wrong name, you're given the wrong name." Orchid smiled. "Let's give you a new one."

The red dread warmed Dorothy's neck. Orchid's smile had spread to Greyson and now they were both staring at her.

"What name do you think you should have had?" Orchid asked.

Dorothy glanced toward the cafeteria window again.

"I don't know." She swallowed. "I've always been Dorothy."

"Okay," Orchid said. "We'll come up with something else. What's your last name?"

"Doucet," Dorothy said.

Orchid narrowed her eyes and stared into the sky, as if Dorothy's new name was hovering up there. Dorothy tried to conjure some nicknames for herself, but her mind went blank. So, she waited.

Orchid snapped her fingers again. "I got it!" she said, beaming. "*Didi!* It's a great name, isn't it? Because your first and last name begin with *D*."

Dorothy mentally tried it on.

Didi. Didi. Didi. Didi.

Orchid tapped her index finger against Dorothy's knee. "You look like a Didi. Doesn't she, Greyson?"

Greyson didn't answer at first. He was waiting to see how Dorothy felt about it. She could tell that by the way he was looking at her. After being best friends for seven years, they knew every nuance of each other's expressions.

Dorothy smiled. She hadn't planned to. She just did.

"I like Didi," Dorothy said.

"We just have to decide if it's spelled D-E-E-D-E-E or D-I-D-I," Orchid said.

"I like D-I-D-I," Dorothy replied quietly.

"Me, too," Greyson said.

"Me, too," Orchid said.

❧ *13* ❧

After school, Dorothy—*no, no, Didi,* she reminded herself—followed Greyson out the front doors, as always. The humidity had sneaked back into the air while they were in their afternoon classes. Dorothy mirrored Greyson's slow pace down the front steps, knowing that he liked to give Trevor as much of a head start as possible on the walk home. Trevor didn't pay much attention to either of them—tenth graders didn't have much business with seventh graders, even in a school as small as theirs—but anytime there was an opportunity to create space between them, Greyson took it, which meant Dorothy took it, too.

She walked to his right because that's how they'd always walked. Her house was six blocks away; Greyson's was eight. The journey home was lined with woods on one side—woods that separated the school and the road from the towering smokestacks of Gimmerton Chemical—and small, quiet neighborhoods on the other. Just beyond the neighborhood of single-family homes was Fox Run, the town's lone trailer park. That's where the God Squad lived—Daelyn, Hallie, and Baylee, who all went to First Baptist in Grand Saintlodge—as well as Max and Daniel, the guys who played football with Michael Colt.

"There's a football game this weekend in Grand Saintlodge," said Dorothy as they reached the bottom of the steps. "We haven't been to a game in a while. My dad could drop us off."

Neither of them was really interested in watching the game, but the youth football league in Grand Saintlodge played almost every weekend next to Crosby Park and students from Fawn Creek often went, just because it was something to do. Dorothy and Greyson had the same routine for every game: as soon as the first quarter started, they bought armfuls of chips, popcorn, and push-up pops from the high schoolers at the concession stand and lugged their haul to their favorite out-of-the-way picnic table. They'd never actually *watched* any football.

"I'm going duck hunting this weekend," Greyson said. "Maybe I'll go after."

Dorothy stopped. Kids splintered off left and right around them, moving toward their neighborhoods.

"Duck hunting?" she said.

There was nothing strange about a boy from Fawn Creek, Louisiana, going duck hunting. But there was certainly something strange about *this* boy going duck hunting. Dorothy knew there was not a single cell in Greyson's body that had any desire to trudge through the marsh to kill ducks.

"I can't get out of it," Greyson said. "It was bound to happen sooner or later."

Dorothy was about to argue with him when Orchid appeared over Greyson's shoulder. She descended gracefully down the steps and waved at Dorothy.

Simile: she moved like a butterfly.

Dorothy smiled shyly and waved back.

Before Greyson could turn around, Orchid had her hands over his eyes. Dorothy counted the bracelets on her wrists. Three on each.

"Guess who?" Orchid chirped.

"Kate Middleton," Greyson said.

Orchid dropped her hands and said, "Close enough!" She smiled and adjusted the strap on her backpack. There was a small pin attached to it—a monkey.

"I like your pin," Greyson said.

"Me, too," Dorothy said.

"Thank you! I got it in Thailand last year," Orchid said. She looped one hand in the crook of Greyson's arm and the other in Dorothy's. They walked together down the sidewalk. Students passed, eyeing Orchid, eyeing all three of them. Dorothy felt regal, walking with Orchid like that.

"Thailand?" Greyson said. "I thought you said you were in Paris."

"I was. And before that—Thailand." Orchid turned to Dorothy. "So, Didi, what were you two talking about?"

"Duck hunting," Dorothy said.

Orchid scrunched her nose.

"You've been to Thailand *and* Paris?" Greyson said.

Orchid shrugged with one shoulder. "Thailand, Paris, London, Iceland—"

"Iceland!" Dorothy said.

"What's it like in Iceland?" Greyson asked.

Orchid thought about this. "Icy," she finally said.

They approached the first crosswalk. On a normal day, the students who lived in the trailer park, or on any of the streets one block west of school, would be waiting for Miss Pam, the crossing guard, to accompany them across the two-lane road, anxious to get home. But today, a small group was gathered. Max and Daniel stood on either side of Colt, who towered over them, the tallest kid in seventh grade. Max had long, wavy hair that the girls—most recently, Janie Crawford—gushed over. (When it was particularly hot outside, his waves turned into long, drippy ropes, which Dorothy thought was disgusting.) Daniel had a crop of curly red hair. In elementary school, people teased him about it, but he didn't care. He said he was "proud to have a flame brain."

All three of them were looking at Dorothy.

Well, not Dorothy.

Orchid.

"Hey, Orchid," Colt said, half waving.

Dorothy, Greyson, and Orchid, still arm in arm, stopped.

"Hi," Orchid said. She didn't put her head down, the way Dorothy did when people unexpectedly spoke to her. She looked right at Colt. Then at Max and Daniel.

"We, uh . . . " Colt looked away. Glanced at Dorothy and Greyson. Back at Orchid. "We just wanted to tell you about our football game this weekend." He wagged a thumb between himself and his two friends. "We're playing in Saintlodge."

"What is Saintlodge?" Orchid asked.

"It's the next town over," Daniel offered. "Dorothy and Greyson go to the games sometimes. They can tell you where it is. You know. If you're curious, or whatever."

Orchid looked at Greyson and raised her eyebrows, as if to ask: *Is this true?*

Greyson shrugged.

"You should come," Colt said. "You know. All three of you."

"Maybe," Greyson said.

Orchid looked at Dorothy. "Are you going to the game, Didi?"

Dorothy's cheeks warmed. She liked being called Didi. She liked standing next to Orchid.

"Maybe," Dorothy said.

Orchid turned back to the three guys. "Maybe," she said.

"Cool," Colt said. "I mean, if you can't, it's no big deal."

"Yeah, it's no big deal," Max repeated. "We just thought we'd ask."

"Okay," Orchid said. She continued down the sidewalk. Dorothy and Greyson followed her lead. She called, "See you tomorrow!" over her shoulder.

"Who are those guys?" Orchid asked once they were out of earshot.

"Michael Colt, Max Bordelon, and Daniel Landry," Greyson replied. "Michael is the tall one. Everyone calls him Colt. Max had the long hair. And Daniel had the red hair."

Dorothy wondered how someone would describe their trio. *Orchid is the beautiful girl. Greyson is the boy. And Dorothy's the other one.*

"They play football," Dorothy added. "They're okay, I guess. We never really talk to them."

"In a place as small as this, it seems like you'd have to talk to everybody," Orchid said.

Greyson huffed. "Not if we can help it."

The second corner—where Greyson and Dorothy always crossed—was up ahead. Orchid stopped suddenly and turned to them.

"You'll have to give me all the details on who's who in Fawn Creek," she said. "Maybe tomorrow at lunch?"

Greyson and Dorothy nodded.

"Great!" Orchid said. "I'll catch up with you tomorrow, then."

It sounded like a farewell, but this was a strange place to part ways.

"Where—?" Greyson started to ask, but Orchid interrupted him with a kiss on both cheeks, which she also gave Dorothy, like they were actors in an old movie.

"Where do you live?" Greyson continued, but Orchid had already darted off into the grass and was running toward the thick woods.

Greyson and Dorothy looked at each other, silent and confused.

There were no houses that way.

Nothing but endless trees shielding the stacks of Gimmerton Chemical.

❀ *14* ❀

At the beginning of the school year, Mr. Agosto told his seventh graders that storytelling was an ancient global tradition that existed long before paper was invented. According to Mr. Agosto, oral storytelling was a special skill, and storytellers traveled far and wide just to share their gift. People would gather around to listen and escape their daily troubles. At the time, Greyson thought it sounded boring. A life without YouTube, movies, or reality television? Just sitting around, listening to some random person talk? No thank you.

But now, here he was, sitting cross-legged on the long-abandoned basketball court behind the cafeteria, waiting to hear a story. But not a tall tale or a fairy tale.

This was a *true* story, straight from the source.

Dorothy sat next to him, also waiting, also looking at Orchid.

They'd eaten their lunch in a hurry so they could come outside. Orchid had just taken a bite of her apple when Greyson asked about Paris.

"Paris," Orchid said as she chewed. A faraway look blanketed her face, like she was remembering something sad from long ago. A butterfly fluttered over from the grass. It lingered around Orchid's head and landed on her shoulder but was gone before Greyson could remark on it. She swallowed. "It's difficult to talk about."

"Why?" Dorothy asked.

Orchid looked at her lap. "Because of Victor."

"Who's Victor?" asked Greyson.

"My boyfriend. Sort of. He's French, of course. Not many people at my old school spoke English except for him, and he spoke it with an accent." She looked up and smiled. "Like, instead of saying 'lettuce,' he'd pronounce it 'lay-toosh'!" She took another bite of her apple, then threw it, half-eaten, into the grass.

Greyson and Dorothy both repeated it—"Lay-toosh! Lay-toosh!"—and laughed.

"We liked to make fun of each other's accents, but we also liked to teach each other new words," Orchid continued. She sighed. "I miss him."

"My dad speaks some French," said Greyson. "Cajun French. He used to speak it sometimes with his grandparents before they died."

"Cajun French is different from real French," Dorothy said.

"Both of them are real French, Didi," Orchid said, not unkindly. "Anytime people speak a language of their own, it's real. Just different."

Sometimes Orchid sounded like an adult trapped inside a twelve-year-old. Greyson wondered if that's what happened when you traveled the world. You became more mature and learned how to sound sophisticated, maybe.

"How did you talk to people if they didn't speak English?" Greyson asked.

"That's what's great about Paris *and* New York," Orchid said. "There are so many different kinds of people speaking all different languages. The best thing about big cities is the people. You can be whoever you want. You could wear a flamingo on your head on Fifth Avenue, and no one looks twice!"

Greyson wondered what it would be like to see people from all over the world, with different stories and histories and customs. In Fawn Creek everyone was from the same place—right here. They had all lived in Fawn Creek for generations. They watched college football on Saturdays, went to church on Sundays, and worked at Gimmerton when they grew up.

"Sounds a lot more exciting than Yawn Creek," Dorothy said.

"There are good things about small towns, too," Orchid said. "My dad says you can find something good in anything, if you look hard enough."

"You sound like one of my mother's pillows again," Greyson said.

Orchid smiled. "It's true! For example, people look out for one another in small towns."

Greyson thought about the bruise on his arm, which had faded to a disgusting yellow. The color of a banana that was just about to turn bad.

"That's not true in Fawn Creek. No one looks out for me here but Dorothy," Greyson said.

"Didi," Dorothy corrected. She laid her head on Greyson's shoulder. "And no one looks out for me but Greyson."

"I bet more people are looking out for you than you think," said Orchid.

A dozen thoughts flew through Greyson's mind. Mostly that Orchid was hopelessly naive and optimistic. *Maybe that's what happens when you get to travel everywhere,* he thought.

You start to think people are good, even when they're not.

"Tell us more about Victor," Dorothy said.

"Victor," Orchid repeated. "Let's see . . . " She looked up into the blue, blue sky and blinked. "He had brown hair that sometimes fell over one eye. He would always flick it away, like this." Orchid demonstrated. "And his eyes were brown, too. A beautiful brown. The color of chestnuts."

"I've never thought of brown eyes as beautiful," Dorothy said.

Of the three of them, she was the only one with brown eyes.

"There are so many beautiful brown things!" Orchid said, her voice pitched with incredulity. "Chestnuts! Trees! Violins!"

"Brand-new leather boots!" Greyson added. "Gingerbread!"

Dorothy's neck turned a light shade of pink.

Orchid continued, even louder: "Mahogany! Teddy bears!"

"Zucchini!" Greyson said, still louder.

Orchid opened her mouth to shout another string of beautiful brown items, then looked at Greyson and said, "Wait a minute, zucchini isn't brown."

Dorothy's face was full-on red now, but she was smiling.

"He meant his dog," Dorothy said.

"She's a chocolate Lab," Greyson clarified.

Orchid laughed, threw both arms in the air, and hollered, "Zucchini! Zucchini! Zucchini!"

To Greyson's surprise, Dorothy tossed back her head and joined in.

"Zucchini! Zucchini! Zucchini!" Dorothy cried.

Greyson stayed quiet and watched them.

He felt light enough to float away.

15

Mr. Shaughnessy was preoccupied with a table of third graders. Figured. All kinds of noise coming from outside, and he wasn't even *monitoring*. Wasn't that what a lunch monitor was supposed to do? *Monitor* stuff? Janie shook her head at the injustice but kept her eyes on the window. Those three were becoming thick as thieves, weren't they, sitting outside together and leaving school together and all that? "Thick as thieves" was something her daddy liked to say about her and Abby. *The two of you are thick as thieves,* he'd say. And Janie liked the way it sounded, because she liked the idea of being a thief—not really stealing anything, mind you, but there was something exciting about the thought of being a villain, even if she wasn't. She was much too nice to be a bad guy. But it was fun to think about.

The noise from the abandoned basketball court swelled and swelled. It was like they didn't even care that they weren't supposed to be out there.

Janie glanced back at Mr. Shaugnessy. He was turned away, still fussing at the little ones. She spotted Max Bordelon sitting with Colt and Daniel at their usual table. They were looking at something on Daniel's iPad and laughing. Max had the greatest laugh.

When he looked up, Janie quickly looked away and focused on her own table.

Abby, Barn, and Slowly were engaged in some ridiculous conversation about the upcoming fall dance in Grand Saintlodge. Abby was chomping an enormous piece of gum and wondering if she would meet anyone new. Meaning new *boys*.

Normally Janie would be invested in the conversation, but right now, she wanted to get to the bottom of what was happening outside on the basketball court.

"I'm going out there," she announced.

"Out where?" Slowly said.

"Out there." Janie motioned toward the window and stood up. "I want to see what they're up to."

"Why?" Slowly asked.

Janie put her hand on her hip. "Why not?"

Slowly shrugged.

"Is anyone coming with me?" Janie asked, scanning their faces. "We've got to go now, while Mr. Shaughnessy isn't looking."

"It's too hot," said Barn. He'd dropped a bite of peach cobbler on his shirt, so now there was a wet glob right in the center of his chest, like a bull's-eye.

"Well, *I'm* going," Janie said. After she got rid of her lunch—seriously, would this school *ever* have appetizing food?—she casually walked toward the back door. She passed the boxes of napkins and straws and wondered if the alarm would sound when she pressed on the push bar to go outside. But it hadn't sounded before, and it didn't sound for her, either. She had the door halfway open when Abby and Slowly caught up to her.

They stepped into the blazing Louisiana sun and headed through the tall grass toward the basketball court. Orchid, Dorothy, and Greyson were quiet and leaning forward, like a huddle. They straightened up when they saw Janie, Abby, and Slowly. Orchid smiled widely. Greyson and Dorothy didn't, which Janie thought was rude; who did they think they were, scowling at *her*? Couldn't a person walk outside anymore? It's not like the three of them owned the stupid basketball court.

"Hello!" Orchid chirped.

Janie squinted down at her. "What's going on out here?" She sounded more forceful than she'd intended. She sounded like her mother. That's not how she'd meant to sound, but sometimes words came out of your mouth and there's nothing you could do about it. She'd intended to sound more casual, like *Hey, just curious what you were talking about because it looked like you were having an interesting conversation,* but that's not why she'd come outside, was it?

Whatever.

Orchid's smile dimmed. "We're just talking."

"About what?" Abby asked. She blew a bubble. The air exploded with the scent of strawberry Bubbalicious.

"About *none of your business,*" Greyson said, his eyes narrowed.

Greyson was such a pill sometimes. That's a word her aunt Kiki used. And that's exactly what Greyson was—a pill. Ever since Janie and Abby accidentally-on-purpose started that rumor about him at the beginning of last year, Greyson acted like he couldn't be bothered with them or something. *Hello, Greyson, get over it, it's been like a million years since all that happened and it's time to move on with your life,* Janie thought.

But she didn't say that, because she was "minding her

Southern manners," as her maw-maw liked to say.

"We were just curious, Greyson, geez," Abby said.

Smack. Smack. Smack.

"I wasn't curious at all," Slowly said. "I was just bored."

Abby jerked her head toward him. "Then why did you come out here, Slowly? Nobody forced you. God."

Orchid looked at Slowly. "I thought your name was Lehigh," she said, smiling kindly. "I'm trying to remember everyone's name."

Slowly opened his mouth to reply, but Janie spoke instead. There wasn't much time left for lunch, and she didn't want to waste it talking about Slowly, of all people.

"His name *is* Lehigh. Lehigh *Kingery*. But no one calls him that," Janie said. "We heard y'all yelling out here, so we came to see what all the fuss is about."

The sun moved across Orchid's face. She shielded her eyes with her hand. "I was just telling Greyson and Didi about—"

"Who?" asked Janie.

"Who what?" Orchid replied.

"Greyson and who?"

Dorothy tilted her head forward so her hair hid part of her face. You'd think Dorothy Doucet would be able to talk to people after knowing them for her *entire life*, but once she'd started middle school, it's like someone had stitched the girl's mouth closed and told her to hide behind a wall of hair.

Pathetic.

"Didi," Orchid said. "Otherwise known as Dorothy."

"Didi," Slowly repeated. "That's a good nickname."

Janie shot him a look that said *Shush.*

"I agree," Orchid said. "But it's not as unique as yours. I've never heard of an adverb used as a nickname."

"An adverb?" Slowly repeated. "Yeah, I guess I never thought of it like that. An adverb."

Abby snorted. "You don't even know what an adverb is." *Smack. Smack. Smack.*

"Yes, I do," Slowly said.

"How did you manage to get an adverb for a nickname?" Orchid asked.

Janie sighed. Ugh. Were they seriously going to talk about *Slowly* this whole time?

"We call him Slowly because he used to be slow," Janie said.

Greyson snickered and mumbled, "Used to be?"

Orchid's eyes snapped to Greyson. Her smile disappeared. She looked from Greyson to Janie to Abby to Slowly. She dropped her hand to her lap. The sun lit up her face.

Is she seriously judging us? Janie thought. *She's here for five minutes and she already thinks she's better than us? It's not like we're being mean. Everyone has nicknames around here. So what. I call Renni a loser sometimes, and she knows I'm not serious. So what. So what.*

"It's interesting to have an adverb as a nickname, but I think Lehigh sounds even lovelier," Orchid said. "Do you mind if I call you Lehigh, Lehigh?"

Slowly shrugged. "Sure."

Did she really just say "Lehigh sounds even lovelier"? Who talks like that? What is she, eighty years old? Does she *like* him or something? No way. No one as pretty as Orchid would like someone like Slowly.

Not that I think she's that pretty, Janie clarified to herself.

"So . . . " said Janie. "Finish your sentence. You were just telling Greyson and *Didi* what?"

Finish your sentence. That's something Renni would say.

"I was telling them about my first kiss," Orchid said.

Slowly groaned. "Ugh. I'm going back in."

The words had barely left his mouth when the bell rang.

❀ *16* ❀

Greyson thought about that look Orchid had given him. He tried to shake it off as they snuck back into the building and gathered their things for earth science, but it kept replaying in his mind over and over and over.

She didn't understand, that was all. She didn't know Slowly or the others. She'd only been at Fawn Creek for five days. Fawn Creek wasn't Paris or New York. People had nicknames here; people had histories. Slowly didn't even care that people called him that. And besides, Slowly had called Greyson plenty of names himself, especially after Janie and Abby started that rumor about him last year.

Orchid didn't *know* Slowly. She didn't *know* the Crawford girls. She thought the world was all bright and beautiful, but that's not how things worked all the time, especially not here.

Greyson wanted to say something, wanted to defend himself, as the three of them walked together to Mrs. Ursu's classroom. But Dorothy (*Didi*, he reminded himself) was listening to Orchid talk about Victor. They'd kissed at a place called the Love Lock Bridge. Apparently it was a famous tourist attraction. Couples hooked padlocks on the bridge, then threw the keys into the Seine River. It was a way for people to pledge their eternal love to each other.

"We didn't have a padlock, but it didn't matter," Orchid was saying. "He knew I was leaving, and he wanted to give me my first kiss before I left."

Dorothy—Didi—said something about that being romantic, but Greyson didn't care about romance or first kisses or lock bridges or anything at that moment, because he kept thinking about that look.

By the time they reached earth science and sat down at the wide tables, Greyson had decided that he'd done nothing wrong. Slowly had called *him* names plenty of times and didn't deserve any sympathy. That's what he decided. Orchid would learn soon enough how things worked in Fawn Creek.

Maybe sooner rather than later, because Mrs. Ursu announced that they would have lab partners for their class period and, to their horror, she would be the one to assign them.

"We have thirteen students now, which is an odd number. That means one of you will be paired with yours truly." She opened her arms wide. "Lucky, lucky."

Mrs. Ursu wasn't that bad as far as teachers went, so none of them would have really minded being paired with her. A more perfect scenario would have allowed them to pick their own partners, but Greyson had learned not to expect perfect scenarios.

Mrs. Ursu explained that they would be studying density and then got to the more important order of business: assigning partners. She cast her eyes over them.

Greyson knew she wouldn't pair him with Didi. That would be too easy. Orchid wouldn't be that bad, but what if she said something about his stupid comment? And why was he still worried about it, anyway?

He hoped for one of the God Squad—Daelyn, Hallie, or Baylee. They were okay, all things considered.

"Colt and Dorothy," Mrs. Ursu said, pointing at one then the other as she partnered them off. She moved quickly after that. "Abby and Max. Orchid and Daelyn. Janie and Daniel. Greyson and Baylee. Hallie and Barn." She motioned to Slowly. "Lehigh, you're with me. You can help me distribute the materials."

❀ ❀ ❀

Abby + Max

It's not my fault I got paired with Max, Abby thought, as she caught the narrowed eyes of her cousin Janie. Besides, she had already decided on a plan of action. She would use this precious time to talk about Janie. She would gauge Max's interest. Maybe after all these years, he'd started to notice Janie just like Janie had noticed him?

Everyone noticed Janie. She was the prettiest girl in school.

Well. The second prettiest, since Orchid arrived.

Not that she'd ever say that to Janie.

"Hey," Max said, flatly.

"Hey."

Abby had to admit, Max had become kind of cute since sixth grade. Maybe he was always cute and she just hadn't noticed. She wasn't sure. But she totally understood what Janie saw in him.

Not that *she* liked Max. Abby had already decided that she was going to meet someone at the dance in Saintlodge. An eighth grader, maybe.

"Are you going to the dance?" Abby asked.

Max's books were neatly stacked at the corner of the table. "What dance?" he said as Mrs. Ursu and Slowly came around to distribute Mason jars.

"There's a dance in Saintlodge the weekend before Thanksgiving break," Abby said.

Max brushed the hair out of his face and pulled the Mason jar between them on the table. "Why would I go to that? I don't go to school there."

"It's not a school thing," Abby replied. "It's being hosted by the city rec. I'm surprised you didn't hear about it."

"When it comes to the rec league, all I care about is football. They probably have sewing classes and ballet, for all I know, but it's not like I'm paying attention. The only thing I have my eye on is the football." He mimicked tossing a football into the air.

Abby tried not to gag.

"Well, anyway, there's a dance, and anyone can go," Abby said. "It's only five dollars to get in."

Mrs. Ursu and Slowly came around again, this time with small bottles of dishwashing liquid from the Dollar Tree.

Max placed the bottle directly next to the Mason jar.

"You could even ask someone, if you wanted," Abby said.

Max snorted. "Like who? You?"

The way he said it. *Like who? You?* Like it would be a joke for him to ask her. Where did he get off? She was a Crawford. And she was pretty. Everyone said so. *Everyone.*

"No, doofus," Abby said. "Like Janie."

Max snorted again. Abby had the sudden urge to smack him over the head, but instead she took the bottle of vegetable oil Slowly handed her and placed it next to the Mason jar and dishwashing liquid.

"No thanks," said Max. He made a face like he'd just eaten something sour.

"What do you mean, 'no thanks'?" Abby said. She crossed her arms.

"No offense, but your cousin is kind of the definition of a *dumb blonde*."

Now Abby really wanted to smack him. "Excuse me?" she said.

Max shrugged. "I said 'no offense.'"

"My cousin is the prettiest girl in school," Abby said. "You're lucky she would even consider going with you."

"Looks are overrated," Max said. "Besides, she kinda looks like a horse." He paused. "No offense."

Abby wanted to conjure up a really clever comeback. Something truly harsh and biting.

But her mind was blank.

Greyson + Baylee

Greyson stared at the dishwashing liquid. He wished he was at home, sitting with Zuke in the backyard.

"So what's she like?" Baylee asked.

Greyson turned to her. Baylee had started wearing pink lipstick that matched the rubber bands on her braces.

"Who?" Greyson said, absently.

"Orchid," Baylee said, half-whispering and glancing in Orchid's direction. "I haven't really talked to her yet."

"Oh," Greyson said. "She's great."

"Is it true that she lived in New York and Paris?"

"Yeah. She was telling us about Paris at lunch."

"Is that what y'all were talking about outside?"

"Pretty much."

Baylee thanked Slowly as he handed her a bottle of rubbing alcohol. After Slowly walked off, she said, "Is it true that she's in witness protection?"

"What? No." *At least I don't think so.*

Baylee sighed. "I wish I could go to Paris. It's one of the cities on my list."

"What list?"

"The list of places I want to visit."

"Oh." Greyson paused. "You should sit outside with us next time. She'll tell you all about it. She's even been to Iceland and Thailand."

"Wow," Baylee said.

"Are they on your list?"

"Not yet."

They stared at the Mason jar, dishwashing liquid, vegetable oil, and rubbing alcohol in front of them. But there were more materials on the way, apparently. Slowly and Mrs. Ursu were moving down the aisle again.

"What places are on *your* list?" Baylee asked.

Greyson stared at the bottle of red food coloring that Slowly placed in front of him.

"Everywhere," he said.

Hallie + Barnet

Hallie leaned over and whispered, "So what do you think of the new girl?" She twisted her hair into a bun on top of her head and stuck a pencil through it to hold it in place. She was wearing her favorite T-shirt, the one that said "Jesus Is My Boo" in spooky letters. Daelyn and Baylee said it was time to retire the shirt now that Halloween was over, but she loved it almost as much as she loved Jesus and puns.

"What do you mean?" Barn said. He had a big stain on his shirt. Classic Barn. Hallie tried not to look at it.

"I don't know," Hallie said. "She seems interesting. That's all."

"I guess," Barn said.

"She's from New York. What do you think a girl from New York is doing in a place like this?"

"Don't know. Don't care."

"I heard she's in the witness protection program. Like, on the run."

When Slowly came around with the Mason jars, Barn pretended he was going to trip him. Both boys laughed like it was the most hilarious thing that had ever happened.

"What are your theories?" Hallie asked.

"My theory is, who cares," Barn said. "What's so great about New York or wherever? People are people no matter where they're from, and I'm from right here."

Hallie sighed. She should have known better than to ask Barnet Kingery for theories.

"If you wanna blab about the new girl, you should talk to Colt," Barn said, nodding his chin toward the back of Michael Colt's head. "I think he's in love with her or something." Barn chuckled at this.

"Really?" Hallie said. "Interesting."

"If you ask me, she looks dirty."

Hallie glanced at the stain on Barn's shirt.

From this angle, it almost looked like Alaska.

Colt + Didi

Michael Colt was the tallest kid in their class, but Dorothy remembered when he was small and scared and cried for his mother. The entire first week of second grade, he'd stood in the doorway and screamed for her to come back while Dorothy watched wide-eyed from the corner, amazed at how loud one person could be. The Doucet house was always quiet, like someone had settled a blanket on top of it and put the noise to bed.

Now Colt was tall and broad shouldered. When he reached over to pull the Mason jar closer to him, his arm seemed impossibly long.

Dorothy moved the other items to the center of the table as Slowly and Mrs. Ursu dropped them off.

"Hey, uh, Dorothy?" Colt said, his voice low. He wiped his hands on his jeans and glanced in Orchid's direction. "Can I ask you something?"

The red dread threatened to crawl up her neck. She tried to imagine Colt as that teary-eyed and screaming second grader. That's what Greyson had told her to do when she felt inexplicably shy.

"You know them," Greyson had said, more than once. "All of them. Just think of an embarrassing moment that you remember. Like when Barn wet his pants."

It usually worked for about two seconds, until she remembered that they also knew *her* embarrassing moments.

"Sure," Dorothy said. She kept her eyes on the Mason jar.

She had a feeling she already knew the question, anyway.

"Does Orchid have a boyfriend?" he asked.

Slowly brought a small container of honey to their table. It was shaped like a bear.

Dorothy thought about Orchid's French boyfriend Victor. Their kiss on the lock bridge.

"Not really," Dorothy said.

"What does 'not really' mean?"

"Well. She had a boyfriend in France before she got here. His name is Victor," Dorothy replied. Colt leaned forward to hear her. People did that sometimes, and she would try to talk more loudly, but it never seemed loud enough. "But I think they broke up."

Colt raised his eyebrows.

No one had ever come to her with questions like this before.

Dorothy Doucet never had valuable information.

But today she did.

She liked the way it felt.

"Oh," Colt said. He absently squeezed the honey bear. "Well." He paused. "Do you think y'all will go to the game this weekend?"

Dorothy—Didi—shrugged. "Maybe," she said, surprised at how casual she sounded. "We haven't decided yet."

We.

She liked how that word sat on her tongue. *We.* It felt like a big, important word for just one syllable.

We.

Me and Orchid.

Or was it Orchid and I?

"Maybe you could talk to her for me," Colt said. "Me and the guys were thinking about going to that dance thing in Saintlodge."

Dorothy didn't say anything.

"I mean, I'm not saying I'm gonna *ask* her to go, like, *with* me or whatever, but if she's going—if y'all are going—it might be cool to meet up or something." He shrugged.

Dorothy turned to him. The room felt charged, like everything and nothing had changed.

"Maybe," she said.

Janie + Daniel

Daniel picked up the bottle of honey, held it next to his face, and said, "Janie Crawford, will you be my honey?" in the same singsongy voice that he used for his baby sister at home.

It wasn't the funniest joke in the world—or even in the classroom—but Janie laughed loudly like he was some great comedian. She wasn't fooling him, though. He knew she liked Max. She kept looking Max's way for one thing, even when Daniel was speaking, which was kinda rude, but he didn't much care. Janie Crawford was stuck-up in his personal opinion, but maybe he'd be stuck-up too if he lived in a big house instead of a run-down trailer that smelled like feet.

"You're so funny!" Janie said.

"I am here to entertain." Daniel put the honey bear back in its original place.

After a few moments of silence, Janie said, "Sooooooo . . . " She dragged out the *o*. "Are y'all going to that dance in Saintlodge?" She sighed dramatically. "It sounds kinda boring, but there's nothing else to do."

It annoyed Daniel when people called things boring even if they didn't really *think* they were boring, just so they sounded cool. But this was the way of the world, so he played along and said, "Maybe."

Janie was looking at Max again. "Do you think y'all will bring dates or anything?"

"Dates?" Daniel repeated, as if she was speaking another language.

Slowly and Mrs. Ursu were distributing Dixie cups full of water now. Slowly spilled a few drops as he set one on their table.

"Yeah," Janie said. "I mean. I think some people are bringing dates."

"I don't know. Maybe Colt will ask that Orchid girl."

"What about Max?"

"I don't think he's gonna ask Max."

Janie sighed again, this time frustrated. "You know what I mean."

"All I know for certain is that I'm not going with anyone. Although Ms. Salto was looking *pretty sharp* this morning." He wagged his eyebrows up and down.

Ms. Salto was the sixth-grade social studies teacher. She was approximately two hundred years old, according to Daniel's estimates.

Janie laughed—again, too loudly. Then she lowered her voice and said, "Do you really think Colt is going to ask Orchid?"

"Who knows. The man is a mystery wrapped in an enigma." Daniel shrugged. "What do you care, anyway?"

But she wasn't listening anymore because she was texting under the table.

Orchid + Daelyn

Last year Daelyn Guidry went on a mission trip to Costa Rica with her youth group at the Baptist church in Grand Saintlodge. Baylee and Hallie were also in the youth group, but neither of them could afford the trip. Daelyn went, though, and she did the Lord's work—at least in her calculations.

She was the only seventh grader at Fawn Creek who had ever traveled outside of the United States. Some of the other kids had pummeled her with questions when she returned, which she'd answered truthfully. For the most part.

She *may* have invented an innocent, daylong romance with a local boy. Let's face it: the audience wanted something interesting, and her actual day-to-day mission life wasn't the most exciting narrative in the world. She spent much of her time washing clothes, preparing food, and spreading the good word. It wasn't the grandiose adventure her classmates had imagined.

But now she was sitting next to someone who'd actually *had* grandiose adventures.

"What's it like in New York City?" Daelyn whispered as Slowly set a bottle of dishwashing liquid on their table.

Orchid smiled. She had a shiny smile with perfectly straight teeth. Daelyn's braces suddenly felt like the ugliest things in the world.

"I love New York," Orchid said. "There are always crowds rushing around, and you hear all different kinds of languages. There are people there from all over the world.

You always see something new. And the food!" Orchid licked her lips. "You can get any kind of food you want at any time."

"Like what?"

"Like chicken shawarma. Falafel. Samosas. Pancit. Lumpia. Kefta and couscous." Orchid licked her lips again, like she'd just ordered a huge plate of all these things (none of which Daelyn had ever heard of) and she was waiting for them to be delivered. "And—of course—pizza! New York is famous for its pizza. There was this one little place on the corner that I used to walk to."

Daelyn had definitely heard of pizza.

"There's only one place to get pizza here," Daelyn said. "You have to order it from King's."

"What's King's?"

"It's the gas station. It's owned by the Kingerys. Everyone calls it King's." She glanced toward Barn and Slowly, then whispered, "The pizza is terrible and they don't even deliver."

"One place for pizza?" Orchid frowned, as if this was the saddest thing she'd ever heard.

"What toppings would you get?" Daelyn asked.

"When you eat New York pizza, you should always choose plain cheese, in my opinion," Orchid said.

"I went to Costa Rica last year," Daelyn said. She hadn't

planned on saying it, but it fell out of her mouth. She wanted to have something to offer to the conversation. "We ate mostly rice and beans and plantains. They were good."

Orchid smiled wide. Her eyes seemed to sparkle.

"Costa Rica!" Orchid said. "I've never been there. What's it like?"

Daelyn told her about the plane trip and the mission house. She told her about the rice and beans and plantains. She told her about spreading the good word and all the local people she'd met, and how she was relieved that many of them spoke English. She told her about the Bibles they handed out, and how she read passages to some of the little kids as they sat on her lap. She didn't mention the fictional daylong romance.

When she finished, Orchid said, "That sounds lovely."

Daelyn nodded.

Slowly put a bottle of honey on their table.

Daelyn felt self-conscious all of a sudden. Did she sound too braggy? Did Orchid think she was showing off? Time to change the subject.

"Can I ask you a question?" Daelyn asked.

All the lab materials had been distributed, apparently. Mrs. Ursu was straightening up at the front of the classroom with Slowly lingering nearby. This was the pose she usually took just before she gave them a flurry of instructions.

"Sure," Orchid said.

"What do you miss most about New York?"

A strange expression fell over Orchid's face. Daelyn wasn't sure what to make of it.

"You never see the same thing twice," Orchid said. "That's what I miss most."

A moment of silence settled between them. *It must be lonely,* Daelyn thought, *to move to a small, boring place like Fawn Creek after such an exciting life.*

Daelyn leaned over and whispered, "Do you want to come to church with me sometime? I can text you my number."

Orchid paused. "No, thank you. I don't really go to church. But it's very kind of you to invite me." She smiled. "I don't have a phone, anyway. My dad is weird about that sort of thing."

Daelyn frowned. "How do you keep in touch with your friends, then?"

But Orchid didn't answer, because Mrs. Ursu had started talking.

❀ ❀ ❀

Slowly + Mrs. Ursu

Slowly wasn't smart. He knew that. He wasn't *book smart,* anyways. He'd flunked a couple things. He didn't figure stuff out so fast. Sometimes when he looked at sentences or numbers, it all seemed a mysterious language that everyone spoke but him.

Slowly wasn't smart. But he wasn't dumb, either. Sure, he had almost flunked fourth grade. And he'd flooded the classroom that one time. But what about when he made a B on his ELA paper? Or guessed exactly what time it was without looking at a clock?

People only noticed when he did stupid things. *Slow* things. And when folks made up their mind about someone or something, they usually only saw what they wanted to see.

He considered this a very *smart* observation.

So, he figured, why make B's at all? Just forget about it instead. It wasn't getting him anywhere, anyways. Besides, he had plenty to be proud of. He was a Kingery. His family name was on a big sign on top of the bait and tackle shop. He saw that sign every day. "Kingery Bait and Tackle," it said.

That was him.

Well.

Kind of.

"Lehigh, are you paying attention?" Mrs. Ursu asked.

He realized that she'd been giving instructions to the class while his mind wandered. This was just the sort of thing that got him into trouble sometimes. His mind would walk off and get lost.

The others were already hunched over their Mason jars, getting to work. Slowly had been staring blankly at Hallie Romero's backpack. No reason, just something to look at. She had a pin on it. Jesus in an airplane with "Jesus Is My Copilot" underneath.

"Sure, Mrs. Ursu," Slowly said, even though he hadn't been paying attention at all. Sometimes it was easier to pretend.

"The first step is to drip honey directly in the middle of the jar." She handed him the honey. "Pour slowly and evenly. Don't get any on the sides."

"Maybe you should do it," Slowly said.

He had zero faith that he would be able to pour the honey without getting it on the sides.

"I've made dozens of density columns," Mrs. Ursu said, her eyebrows raised. That was the look she gave them when she thought they were being "'squirrelly.'" (That was her word, not his). "Why would *I* do it?"

Slowly took the honey. He turned it upside down over the jar. Mrs. Ursu adjusted his aim.

"Hold it vertically," she said. "That will help you pour straight."

He squeezed. A thick line of honey trickled out. It moved slower than he expected.

"It's like snot," he said.

"It has more density than snot," Mrs. Ursu said.

So far, so good. The honey moved in slow motion, but none of it had dripped over the sides.

"Once you have a nice little circle, that should be enough," she said. "Like, the size of a nickel."

Slowly liked Mrs. Ursu. She was a good teacher, even if the subject she taught was the most boring topic on planet Earth.

"Mrs. Ursu?" Slowly asked.

A laugh erupted from somewhere, but neither of them looked up. From out of the corner of his eye, Slowly saw Barn lick a dollop of honey off his finger.

"Yes?" Mrs. Ursu paused. "Keep your eye on the honey."

"Can I ask you something?"

"Of course."

"What's an adverb?"

He felt Mrs. Ursu look at him.

"I know it's not a science thing, but I was just wondering what it is," he said. He was suddenly embarrassed and had no idea why. Everyone already thought he was dumb, so what difference did it make if he *sounded* dumb? He wasn't sure.

"An adverb modifies another word," she replied.

Slowly's mouth formed a tight line. He didn't know what "modified" meant.

"When you modify another word, it means that you help describe it," Mrs. Ursu said, as if she'd read his mind. "That should be enough honey."

Slowly tipped the bottle upright and set it down.

He'd done it.

No honey anywhere except where it belonged.

Mrs. Ursu continued. "For example, if I say 'Sally sat in her chair quickly,' the adverb—'quickly'—tells you *how* Sally sat in her chair. Adverbs usually end in 'ly,' like 'quickly' or 'quietly' or 'loudly.' It's just another way to help describe something."

Slowly nodded.

Mrs. Ursu picked up the dish soap and reminded the class what they were doing next. Then she turned to Slowly, lowered her voice, and asked if he had any other questions.

"You can ask, even if it's not a science thing," Mrs. Ursu said.

Slowly thought about this.

"No more questions," he said.

❧ *17* ❧

In a place like Fawn Creek, three things were always certain—heat, humidity, and eavesdroppers. This was especially true at school, where the kids were forced into the same shared space from morning to afternoon, with only a brief respite at lunch (and even then, you weren't spared from meddlers, as proven by Janie's appearance on the basketball court). Because of this, Dorothy wasn't able to tell Orchid about Michael Colt until after school.

She could hardly wait. She could barely contain herself, if you want to know the truth. It was confounding to her that she'd be so excited about news that had nothing to do with her.

She and Greyson waited on the steps. Students spilled

out, all familiar faces in one way or another, though few of them said hello. Not even Colt, who rushed out with Daniel and Max, all of them laughing. Dorothy thought he might say something to her—stop and talk, even—as if they'd bonded or whatever. But he brushed past like always.

"Did you know it hardly ever gets hotter than sixty degrees in Iceland?" Greyson said. He stopped scrolling on his phone for a moment to squint at the relentless Louisiana sun. "I hate the weather here. I wanna move someplace cold. Or at least a place that has *seasons.*"

And finally, here was Orchid, her wild hair collected in a pile. She smiled at them, but before she could get a word out—or even walk down the first step—

"Colt likes you," Dorothy said. She immediately blushed, embarrassed at how quickly and eagerly she'd blurted it out.

Orchid raised her eyebrows. "Which one is he again?"

"The tall one who asked you to the game," Greyson replied. He slipped his phone in his pocket. They descended the steps together.

"I thought he invited all of us," Orchid said.

"Well," Greyson said. "Colt has never cared before if Dorothy and I showed up."

"Didi," Dorothy corrected.

Orchid's smile widened. She looped her arm around

Dorothy's elbow as they walked in unison toward the sidewalk.

"Speaking of names . . . " said Greyson, glancing at Orchid. "Everyone calls him that, you know. It's not a big deal. He doesn't even mind."

"Who?" asked Orchid. "Colt?"

"No. Slowly."

"Oh," Orchid said.

"I'm just saying," Greyson said.

"Okay." Orchid lifted her shoulders. A delicate shrug.

"But what about Colt?" said Dorothy. This was no time to talk of anything else. "Do you like him?"

A group of sixth graders ran past, hurrying to the crosswalk up ahead.

"I don't know anything about him," Orchid said.

"Do you think he's cute?" Dorothy asked.

Another shrug. "I suppose."

"He wants to go to the dance with you," Dorothy said.

At some point Greyson had retrieved his phone again. He walked and scrolled at the same time, even though they were nearing the crosswalk and he was sure to get a stern talking-to from Miss Pam, the crossing guard.

"If you go to the dance with Colt, it will be the scandal of the century," Greyson said.

"Why?" Dorothy and Orchid asked in unison.

Greyson didn't look up. "Two words. Renni Dean."

"What does that mean?" Orchid asked.

They stopped walking and moved out of the way.

Dorothy rolled her eyes. "Renni doesn't even go to this school anymore."

"It doesn't matter," Greyson said. "Janie and Renni are still best friends."

"They broke up," Dorothy said. She had no idea why she was so invested in a successful romance between Colt and Orchid. Really, what did she care? But for some reason, she did. She turned to Orchid to explain. "Colt was Renni's boyfriend last year. But she moved to Saintlodge, so I don't see what the big deal is."

Greyson put his phone back in his pocket. "You obviously don't understand girls."

"Very funny," Dorothy said.

"It doesn't matter, anyway," Orchid said. "I don't want a boyfriend right now."

Dorothy had never thought about whether she wanted a boyfriend or not. Maybe because it never seemed like an option in the first place. "Are you still trying to get over Victor?" she asked.

Orchid paused. "Honestly? Yeah. It's hard to get over someone who says 'lay-toosh' instead of 'lettuce,' after all."

They laughed.

"We should go to the dance together, the three of us," Orchid said. "We'll all be each other's dates." She looked over her shoulder. Toward the field. Toward the distant smokestacks. "I better go. See you tomorrow?"

This time Greyson and Dorothy spoke in unison. "See you tomorrow," they said.

Orchid kissed them each on both cheeks and walked into the grass.

Once she was out of earshot, Greyson said, "Do you think she lives in the woods?"

"Don't know." Dorothy wasn't thinking about where Orchid was going, even as she watched her step through the big, open field.

"People are saying she's in witness protection," Greyson said. "Do you think that's true?"

"Don't know," Dorothy repeated.

She was busying turning over Orchid's words.

The three of us.

Orchid could have been friends with any of the kids at Fawn Creek, but she had chosen Dorothy Doucet and Greyson Broussard.

Dorothy Doucet and Greyson Broussard.

Of all people.

"We should follow her one day," Greyson said.

But Dorothy was too distracted to notice.

❀ *18* ❀

"**T**ell me what he said, word for word," Janie demanded.

Today was Friday, so Janie had heard Abby's account of her conversation with Max several times already. But she got the sneaking suspicion Abby was omitting important details.

She and Abby were sitting cross-legged on Janie's plush, queen-sized bed, which was covered by a teal down comforter and matching pillows. The teal complemented the gray walls, which complemented the curtains, which complemented Janie, who loved to be surrounded by well-balanced color and a clean, tidy room. She couldn't relax in clutter, which is why Abby had Friday night sleepovers at Janie's, rather than the other way around. Abby's room was littered with tank tops, shorts, stuffed animals, hair ribbons, belts, shoes, brushes, you name it.

Abby was *such* a mess sometimes.

"I told you already," Abby said. She fell backward onto the pillows and blinked at the ceiling. "I asked if they were going to the dance and he acted like he didn't know what I was talking about and then he said something dumb about how he only cares about football."

Janie twisted a lock of hair around her finger. "And he never mentioned my name *at all?*"

Abby paused. "No."

"Are you sure?"

"Of course, I'm *sure*. To be honest, I think you can do way better. He used to eat mulch, remember?"

Janie sighed. "That was a million years ago. We were all immature then."

"I'm just saying. You deserve better." Abby sat back up. "Let's go, just the two of us, and we can dance with some eighth graders."

Janie groaned. There were seven eighth-grade boys at Fawn Creek, and none of them were cute. Matt Decker was the only half-decent one, and he was nowhere *near* as cute as Max.

"Not the eighth graders here," Abby said, as if she knew just what Janie was thinking. "The ones from Saintlodge."

They'll be there too, and now we have Renni to introduce us. I bet she knows them. Is she going?"

Hmm.

Maybe Abby was onto something. Janie had been so focused on Max, she hadn't taken time to consider all the possibilities. Saintlodge Middle School wasn't exactly a thriving metropolis, but it certainly had much more to offer than *Yawn* Creek.

"At first she said she wasn't, but when I told *her* what Daniel told *me* about Colt, she decided to 'make an appearance,'" Janie said.

Renni had not been pleased about Colt's interest in Orchid. To say the least.

"Are Colt and Orchid definitely going to the dance together?" Abby asked. Ready for gossip, as always.

"I'm sure she'll say yes if he asks. I mean . . . " Janie raised her hands as if to say, *Why wouldn't she?* Colt was the cutest guy in school. Well, second to Max, of course.

Abby shrugged. "I heard she has a boyfriend in France."

Janie rolled her eyes. "Ugh! I'm *so tired* of hearing about France. It's utterly boring."

"Today at lunch she told us all about Thailand. She said there's a place there called the Phi Phi Islands and it's the most beautiful place she's ever seen, out of all the places in the entire world. There's even a beach where monkeys come right up to you. One of them stole her sandwich. It was a really funny story. She said she had just put down her towel when she heard a noise and—"

"Ugh!" Janie said again. "I don't *care*. It sounds totally made-up. You think a monkey would *seriously* just wander up to someone and take a sandwich? Monkeys don't *do* that. They're, like, wild animals."

Janie hadn't heard the story firsthand because she had refused to go outside. She stayed at the table with Barn and Slowly and watched the other seventh-grade girls—Hallie, Daelyn, Baylee, Dorothy, and eventually, Abby—wander outside to listen to Orchid talk about here and there and everywhere. Frankly, Janie was *over it*. Whoever heard of someone visiting Thailand, anyway? What was she, some kind of CIA agent or something? And if she *was* in the witness protection program like people were saying, it probably meant that she was involved in something bad or illegal.

Janie picked up her phone. "There's something off with that girl," she said, scrolling. "After school she walks into the woods. What's that all about?"

"Maybe her house is that way."

"There aren't any houses over there. You know that. Just woods and Gimmerton." Janie typed "monkey islands Thailand" into Google. Images and links filled her phone.

"Maybe she lives in the woods," Abby offered.

"Don't be stupid," Janie said. "No one lives in the woods."

Abby was so naive sometimes.

"Do you want to go get pizza?" Abby said. "I'm starving!"

Janie expanded her search to "phi phi islands thailand monkeys," and one result after another came up. Images of the most beautiful water Janie had ever seen. White sand beaches. Cliffs that rose up forever. She muted her phone and played one of the videos from Monkey Beach. Little monkeys—no taller than her knees—trotted alongside people on the sand. One man offered a branch to one of them and the monkey latched on to play tug. People gathered all around, smiling and laughing and taking pictures. One of the monkeys grabbed a man's phone and darted away with it.

Okay, so maybe *some* monkeys walked on beaches with humans.

Abby waved her hand in the air. "Hello? What are you looking at? And why are you laughing?"

Had she been? She tucked her smile—and her phone—away. "I'm just looking at something stupid on my phone."

"Do you want to get pizza from King's or what?" Abby said.

"I'd rather eat cardboard from the gutter," said Janie.

❀ *19* ❀

Greyson sat in the sewing room and watched his mother stitch one of her pillowcases. This one said, "A smooth sea never made a skilled sailor," with a little sailboat underneath.

He googled "Paris fashion" on his phone. He'd never thought much about Paris before, but if a girl like Orchid could leave Paris for a place like Fawn Creek, that meant it was possible the other way around, too. Right?

"You all set to go with your dad tomorrow morning?" his mother asked, eyes trained on the pillowcase. "Make sure you're up so he doesn't have to fight you awake. You know how he gets."

Greyson made a noise between discontent and

acknowledgment. Yes, he was "all set" to go duck hunting the next morning—if "all set" meant he was dreading the entire thing like a condemned man dreads his executioner.

"Not like I have a choice," Greyson said.

Images materialized on his phone. Blazers of white fur. Knee-high orange boots. Miniskirts, pantsuits, dresses. Jackets with exaggerated shoulders. Jackets with no shoulders at all.

"You never know—you might enjoy it," his mother continued. "Lord knows your brother does."

"I don't need to go duck hunting to know I won't enjoy it," Greyson said. *But thanks for pointing out that Trevor loves to go. Just another way he is a Great Son and I am the Almost Daughter.* He absently rubbed the place where Trevor had pinched him last week, though all evidence was now gone.

"How do you know if you haven't tried it?"

Greyson looked up from his phone. "Do you need to have your leg amputated to know that you don't want to do it?"

"I hardly think going duck hunting with your father is the same as getting your leg cut off," she said.

If you say so, Greyson thought.

"Maybe you'll have a good time," she said.

She was always trying to convince him—or herself—that he would have a "good time" doing all the things that

Trevor and his father enjoyed. All the things that most guys in town considered a "good time." Fishing, hunting, skinning deer.

Fishing wasn't so bad, though. Greyson could remember his father's giant hands cupped over his tiny fingers, showing him how to bait a hook or reel something in, back when he first learned how to fish. His father's voice had been gentler then, even when Greyson asked if he could throw the fish back instead of letting them die. *You can't do that, kiddo,* his father had said. *It does more harm than good.* Greyson wanted to ask why, but he kept his mouth shut. His father didn't like questions.

Fishing at Fawn Creek was peaceful, almost meditative, even when Trevor was there.

They would each hold their fishing poles and escape into the silence of their thoughts. There was a pleasant *plink* when you cast your line into the water, and a rush of adrenaline when something bit. From far away, they probably looked like a typical family of strong Louisiana men. Two ideal sons with their hardworking father.

"The only way I'll have a good time is if Trevor gets lost in the marsh and we have to leave him behind for the alligators," Greyson said. Usually he said these things quietly to himself, but every now and then, a thought ran away from him.

His mother sat back in her chair and glared at him. "Greyson James Broussard. Don't ever say something like that."

"Sorry," Greyson mumbled, even though he wasn't.

Was it bad to wish your older brother would be eaten by alligators? Maybe. Probably.

His mom was about to say something else when Trevor knocked on the door and immediately opened it. He tossed a package onto the floor near her sewing machine. November was a busy month for her, so she was constantly getting fabric delivered.

"Found that on the porch," Trevor said. He looked down at Greyson. "You excited about going duck hunting, little sister?" He shut the door before Greyson answered.

Not like it was a real question, anyway. And not like Greyson's mom was going to stick up for him. Sure, she'd sometimes tell Trevor to "cut it out," but she never treated it like anything serious, never pretended like it was *cruel*. Brothers tease each other, his parents said. Trevor didn't mean anything by it, they said. They didn't even punish Trevor a few months ago when he called Greyson that word—the one that Greyson couldn't even think about without getting nauseous. *Your brother shouldn't have used that word, but other people are gonna say it, too, if you keep carrying on the way you do,* was all his father said.

Weren't families supposed to look out for one another?

In some other world, maybe.

In this world, Greyson had to look out for himself.

He'd learned that a long time ago.

He turned back to his phone. Wool ponchos in chevron patterns and crocheted gloves with buttons.

"I take back my apology," he said.

Let the gators have him.

❀ *20* ❀

Janie, Abby, and Renni moved through school like bolts of electricity when Renni lived in Fawn Creek. Janie and Abby came from the best-known family in town and Renni's dad had a high-paying job at Gimmerton Chemical—together, they were a force of nature. When Renni announced that her father got a "bigger and better" job and they were moving to Saintlodge, Abby and Janie cried and wailed and sobbed and the trio made a pact that they'd stay best friends no matter what. Janie meant it, for the most part. But there was also a part of her—secret, way deep down—that wanted to celebrate. Not that she'd ever tell anyone. No, she would *never do that.*

Even now, as she and Abby walked up the familiar path to the football field in Saintlodge, Janie experienced a whirl of conflicting emotions. She couldn't wait to see Renni—she was her best friend, after all, her *very best friend*—but a sense of dread loomed over her like a storm cloud. She never felt good after hanging out with Renni. But she liked hanging out with her.

Didn't she?

The city rec football field wasn't much, but it was something. There was a concession stand near the bleachers, and a playground close by, mostly populated by little brothers and sisters. The whole place was already crowded, because Janie had insisted on arriving late.

"There are a lot of people here," Abby said.

Thanks, Queen Obvious, Janie thought.

Abby was right, though. Mostly Saintlodge kids. Hardly anyone from their class at Fawn Creek. Barn and Slowly never came to the football games. The God Squad—Daelyn, Hallie, and Baylee—came sometimes, but today they were off on some Bible-thumping mission. Max, Daniel, and Colt were on the field somewhere.

But there, leaning near the concession stand, were Dorothy Doucet and the new girl.

Janie wondered what had happened to Greyson. Maybe

he'd been sidelined, since Dorothy had an actual friend who was a girl now, instead of a boy who acted like one.

"Let's say hi to Orchid," Abby said, veering in their direction.

"No way," Janie said. "We're meeting Renni."

"So? That doesn't mean we can't say hi."

Sometimes Abby was so dense.

Janie stepped off the walkway onto a patch of green grass. She texted Renni, then shielded her eyes from the sun and scanned the crowd. When Orchid looked their way, Abby waved. The girl just couldn't help herself.

Janie made a point *not* to look in the direction of the concession stand.

She was about to text Renni again when she felt a thump on the back of her head and turned around. It was Renni, of course. For some reason, her preferred method of greeting was to sneak up behind someone and scare the daylights out of them, whether it was a playful shove on the shoulder or a light flick on the skull.

"Hey, losers," Renni said.

She was flanked by two boys—one with brown hair and freckles, the other with blond curls. They were sweating in the sun, holding skateboards.

Abby immediately straightened up and smiled.

Janie straightened up too, but didn't smile. "Hey," she

said. She eyed the boys, then looked at Renni. "Did you just get here?"

"A few minutes ago," said Renni. She pointed to the freckled boy and introduced him as Hunter. The other guy, the blond, was Ethan.

"Hey," Janie said.

"Hey," said Hunter.

"Hey," said Ethan.

Last was Abby. "Hey," she said. "Do you go to Saintlodge?"

"Yeah," Hunter replied. He used his shoulder to rub sweat away from his face. "We're in seventh grade. You?"

Janie had a million questions. Who were these boys? Did Renni like one of them? Did they like her? Why was she with them? Renni hadn't said anything specific about any boys, just *So-and-so is cute* or *Such-and-such keeps staring at me in class.* But Janie didn't remember her mentioning either of these guys.

"They go to Fawn Creek," Renni said to the guys.

"Oh, you're one of *those* kids," Ethan said.

Janie crossed her arms. "What does that mean?"

"Nothing." Ethan shrugged. "Just that you're one of those kids from Fawn Creek. I can usually tell who's a Fawnie just by looking at them."

His friend—Hunter, was it?—chuckled. Renni giggled and swatted Ethan's arm. Clearly, there was an inside joke going on here. Janie did *not* like inside jokes. Particularly those that didn't include her.

"Am I missing something?" she asked.

"Just kidding around," Ethan said, smiling widely. He put his skateboard down. Hunter did the same. "We're taking off. See you around, Renni."

Renni was smiling widely, too. As the boys rolled away, she called out, "Text me later, Ethan!"

"What was *that* all about?" Janie said, rolling her eyes.

Abby put her hands on her hips. "Yeah. What did he mean, 'he can tell just by looking at us'?"

Renni waved it away like it was nothing. "Just Ethan being stupid. That's how he is. He says you can tell who's from Fawn Creek because their parents are usually brother and sister."

Janie arched an eyebrow. "Excuse me?"

What she wanted to say was: *You're from Fawn Creek, too, Renni. Or have you forgotten?*

"Well, *obviously* it's ridiculous, Janie," Renni replied. "It's just his sense of humor." She leaned forward conspiratorially. "Is that girl here? You have to point her out to me."

Janie bristled, then calmed herself. Why harp over

some stupid comment made by an idiot? If Renni wanted to be friends with a person like Ethan, so be it. Plus, if Janie made a big deal about it, then it'd be obvious that she was upset. And even though she *was* upset, she didn't want to *show* that she was upset. People made dumb comments about Fawn Creek all the time. Whatever. She should be used to it by now.

Janie mentally pushed Ethan's smug face aside and turned toward the concession stand. Abby was looking in that direction, too.

"She's right there," Janie said. "The one with Dorothy Doucet."

"Ohmygod. *That's* her?" Renni put her hand to her mouth as if she had just witnessed something truly pitiful. "I thought she'd be way prettier."

Abby frowned and mumbled, "I think she's pretty."

"Maybe to some degree," Renni continued. "But I thought she'd be, like, *really* pretty. She's just kinda average. I can't *believe* Colt likes her."

"Who cares?" Abby said. There was an edge to her voice. Janie knew all of Abby's tones. She was probably still annoyed about Ethan's comment.

Abby took things so seriously sometimes.

"What do you mean, 'who cares'?" Renni said. "Colt is *my* property. And I don't like trespassers."

The three of them were facing Dorothy and Orchid now, making no moves to hide the fact that they were talking about them.

"Let's go say hey," Renni said. "We don't want to be rude."

She started toward the concession stand.

Janie and Abby followed. As always.

21

In the fall of fifth grade, Dorothy lost a tooth. She'd lost several of them by then, of course, but this one was particularly uncomfortable, so she and her mother went to Crawford Grocery to get Orajel. Dorothy was in the pharmacy aisle, looking for the medicine, when someone behind her said, "Boo!" and Dorothy whipped around, heart racing, to find Renni Dean standing there.

It wasn't unusual to run into people in Fawn Creek—in fact, it was inevitable—but Renni and Dorothy had never been friends, even though Mrs. Dean used to cut Dorothy's hair back when Mrs. Dean was a hairdresser. The fact that Renni took the time to approach Dorothy in the supermarket was not a sign of anything good to come. This much, Dorothy knew.

You'd think there'd be nothing to report about a girl in a supermarket, but Renni quickly developed her own theories as to why Dorothy was in the pharmacy aisle. One rumor stuck. Dorothy had boils on her body and was buying cream to remove them. Dorothy didn't even know what a boil was at the time; she'd had to do a Google search, which she immediately regretted. According to Renni, the boils were hidden in private places, which is why none of them were visible. The rumor gained so much momentum that even Greyson had started to suspect it was true. That was the worst part of it. If her best friend in the world believed it, what chance did she have?

Eventually people started gossiping about other things and the story faded and died for everyone but Dorothy, who tensed any time Renni Dean came near her. It was such a relief when Renni moved to Grand Saintlodge that Dorothy and Greyson had shared a celebratory cupcake. But now, here came Renni, with the Crawford cousins on either side, just like the old days.

"Who's that girl with Janie and Abby?" Orchid asked.

Dorothy's voice snagged in her throat. She couldn't speak. She could only watch as the trio of girls got closer and closer. She felt the inklings of red dread prickling her skin.

"Hey, *girls*," said Renni, as if they were children and she was a grown woman. "Where's your pretty boy?"

That's what she called Greyson.

Last year she'd told everyone that Greyson wore makeup and dresses at home. Dorothy remembered the day she'd heard it for the first time. She and Greyson were in his backyard with Zucchini. The dog was nestled against Greyson's face. Greyson's blue eyes sparkled—Dorothy remembered that detail clearly—because he was about to cry. This made Dorothy nervous. In all their years as best friends, she'd never seen Greyson cry. *It's not true, you know*, he'd said. *But so what if it was? So what?*

"'Pretty boy'?" Orchid repeated, like she was trying to work out who Renni was talking about, though Dorothy suspected she knew.

Just go away, Dorothy thought. She willed it into the universe. *Go away, Renni Dean. Go away.*

But Renni was like a cockroach. She always came back.

"*You know*," Renni said. "Trevor Broussard's little brother."

If Dorothy were a different person, she would have rolled her eyes so far back in her head that she'd fall over. Renni was in the same grade as they were, but she referred to Greyson as "Trevor Broussard's little brother," as if she were a sophomore like Trevor.

"Anyway," Renni said. "I heard you're new so I thought I'd introduce myself. My name is Renni—"

"Hi, Renni," Orchid said, smiling tentatively. "My name is—"

"—and even though I don't go to Yawn Creek anymore, you should know that I still have many vested interests at that school."

Orchid's eyes darted from Janie to Abby, who suddenly mumbled that she wanted to get chips and did anyone want to come? But no one was listening, so she just kept standing there.

Orchid said, "Vested interests?"

Renni took a step forward. "Michael Colt."

"Oh," Orchid said. She shrugged. "Okay."

"Okay?" Renni said, scanning Orchid from head to toe, as if appraising a piece of meat.

"Yes. Okay. I don't even—"

"How many birds do you have nesting in that hair, anyway?"

Janie giggled.

Orchid's face went slack. "Actually—"

"I'm going to get chips," Abby announced, walking off. She glanced over her shoulder as she made her way to the concession stand, like the conversation was a train wreck and she couldn't stop herself from witnessing the crash.

But the crash wasn't to be, because Renni turned to Janie and said, "I need to tell you something before Abby gets back. Something *important*." She tugged Janie's sleeve and pulled her away from them. Orchid's unfinished sentence hung in the air, and Dorothy desperately wanted her to finish it.

Actually what? Dorothy wondered. Dorothy had never been able to snap back at Renni. She wanted to know what Orchid would have said. A sarcastic retort? *Actually, I have twelve birds currently nesting.* An insult of equal gravity? *I don't know, Renni. How much air is in your brain?* Something that took the higher road? *Actually, it occurs to me that your insults might be the result of low self-esteem. Is everything okay at home?*

Renni leveled her eyes at Orchid as she and Janie walked away.

❀ *22* ❀

Renni, with a certain look on her face, pulled Janie toward a clearing near the fence. Janie was familiar with this look. It said *I'm about to tell you something bad, but it's for your own good.*

"Abby made me promise not to tell you this, but I think you need to know," Renni whispered.

Janie swallowed and braced herself. "What is it?"

Renni sighed. A big, heavy, dramatic sigh. "It's about Max," she said.

Crowds moved around them, hustling to get food or go to the bathroom or run around on the playground before the game started up again.

"What about him?" asked Janie.

Renni laid a soothing hand on Janie's arm. "I'm only telling you this because I'm your best friend and I don't want to see you embarrass yourself again."

Again? Had Janie embarrassed herself before? When? Janie's heart raced.

"I promised Abby I wouldn't tell you, so you have to promise me you won't tell her that you know," Renni said.

"Know what?"

Renni took a deep breath. "Max told her he doesn't like you. Not in *that* way. Like, at all."

Janie's stomach turned over, a somersault in her belly. Okay, fine. Max Bordelon didn't like her. So what? There were other fish in the sea. Look around. Right here, right now. Boys everywhere. And not just stupid Fawn Creek boys, either.

"Okay," Janie said. "It doesn't matter. I didn't like him that much, anyway. There's plenty of other—"

"That's not all."

Janie's mouth snapped shut.

"He said something else." Renni pressed her lips together. "He told Abby that your looks are way overrated. And . . ."

Janie raised her eyebrows. She could see Abby at the concession stand placing her order at the counter. She was probably getting a corn dog and Diet Coke. That's what she always got.

"And?" Janie said.

If you've got something to say, Renni Dean, then say it.

Renni hesitated and glanced at her sandals. "He said you look like a horse."

Renni pressed her lips together again, presumably because the news was so difficult for her to share, but it also looked to Janie like she wanted to laugh.

No, that's not right.

Sure, Renni could be mean to other people, but they were best friends. She wouldn't think something like that was funny, would she?

A huge bowling ball had lodged itself in Janie's throat and threatened to crash down on her chest, too. She knew this feeling—it's what happened when she was about to cry.

No, no. She couldn't cry in front of Renni. Anyone but Renni.

(But Renni is supposedly your best friend, right? If you can't cry on your best friend's shoulder, who can you cry to, Janie? Who?)

Renni shook her head at the injustice of it all. "Abby should have told you. Sometimes being a good friend means delivering bad news." Janie knew right away why Abby hadn't told her. Because she knew it would crush her. She knew it would embarrass her, so she'd kept it secret. And only told Renni. Of all people.

"Don't tell Abby I told you," Renni said quickly as Abby approached with her corn dog and soda.

Janie wanted to disappear. She wanted to be in her room. She wanted to cover her face—her oval face with its long nose, which she'd always suspected made her ugly, and now she had evidence that she'd been right all along.

When Abby asked if they wanted to find a place in the bleachers to sit down, Janie reached into her back pocket and pulled out her silent phone.

"Someone's calling me," Janie said, feigning surprise. She looked at the lock screen. "It's my mom. Be right back."

She pushed an imaginary button, put the phone to her ear, and broke away as quickly as she could.

❧ *23* ❧

"I think something's wrong with Janie," Orchid said.

Frustration tugged at Dorothy. Before Renni and her minions interrupted them, Orchid had been telling a story about eating éclairs with Victor in the shadow of the Eiffel Tower. Orchid had gotten a smudge of chocolate on her chin and she wasn't even embarrassed. She and Victor laughed about it as they looked up at the bright blue Parisian sky.

"Tell me about it," Dorothy said. She waved her hand dismissively. "So what happened after the éclair? Did you and Victor go back to the lock bridge?"

"I'm serious, Didi." Orchid's eyes were fixed on Janie, who had broken away from Abby and Renni to answer her phone. "She looks upset, and now she's fake talking on her phone."

"Fake talking?"

"Yeah. You know. Pretending to talk to someone when she isn't."

The Eiffel Tower drifted further away.

"She looks like regular Janie to me," Dorothy said. *Regular, irritating, stuck-up, snobby Janie.*

Then again—maybe there *was* something different. Something subtle. But who cared? If something bad had happened to her, she probably deserved it.

Janie wandered toward the concession stand, further away from Renni and Abby and closer to Dorothy and Orchid. She kept the phone to her ear the whole time. It certainly *looked* like a legitimate conversation.

Orchid walked up to her before Dorothy could protest. Not that she would have. Not aloud, anyway.

"Are you okay?" Orchid said, her voice soft.

Janie raised her eyebrows and slipped the phone in her back pocket. Her eyes shimmered, like she was trying not to cry. It reminded Dorothy of that day with Greyson.

"What do you mean, am I okay?" Janie said, her voice laced with scorn. She crossed her arms.

"You look upset, that's all," Orchid said. "I thought

maybe you got bad news or something." She gestured to Janie's pocket.

"It's nothing," Janie said. "Just stupid drama."

"Okay," Orchid said. "Well, I know we don't know each other very well, but if you ever need anything . . . "

Dorothy wondered what Greyson would think if he were here. She'd have to tell him everything as soon as she could. She imagined the text now. *Orchid is fraternizing with the enemy!* Wait—was "fraternizing" the right word?

"Oh," Janie said. Her arms fell to her sides. She glanced at Dorothy. "Thanks, I guess."

"Also, please tell your friend Renni that I'm not going to the dance with Michael Colt. I'm going with Greyson and Didi. A friend date!" Orchid hooked her arm around Dorothy's and smiled. "Do you and Abby want to come with us? It'll be so much fun. It'll be a big friend extravaganza."

Dorothy found herself mumbling, "Yes, but . . . " as her heart raced. When she realized she was speaking aloud, she stopped herself and waited for someone else to say something. Maybe Janie would finish the sentence for her.

Yes, but . . . we're not friends.

"Thanks," Janie said. "But I already have plans."

The mean-girl kick in her voice was gone. She almost sounded like a normal person.

Orchid shrugged. "Just a thought. It'll be fun. No matter what."

"Yeah." Janie smiled. An actual, real-life smile. Well, more like a half smile. It reminded Dorothy of second grade, when Janie broke her pencil and Dorothy had given her a spare. "Thanks, Dorothy," Janie had said. Janie had freckles then, but they were faded now.

Janie turned toward Renni and Abby, who were heading their way.

"See you around," Janie said.

Dorothy lightly pulled Orchid in the opposite direction.

"I hope you don't mind that I invited her to come with us," Orchid said when they were out of earshot. "She just looked upset. I figured she already had plans, anyway. But sometimes it's nice just to be invited."

"Janie's always invited to things," said Dorothy.

They walked toward the playground. During the football games, Dorothy and Greyson spent their time here, sitting on the bench under the oak tree, watching the little kids play, wondering how long it would take before those little kids separated into clusters like they had.

"How could you tell?" Dorothy asked.

"She looked like she was about to cry, so I figured—"

"No. Not that. How could you tell she wasn't really talking to anyone? I couldn't tell."

Orchid shrugged. "Just a feeling."

Their arms were still linked.

"Do you really think we'll have fun at the dance?" asked Dorothy.

"Yes," Orchid replied. "No matter what."

❧ *24* ❧

Greyson did not go duck hunting. Instead, he reverted to a tried-and-true method of avoidance—he faked sick. He considered himself a great actor when it came to phantom illnesses, because he operated under a set of self-imposed rules: Don't use the sick card too often or you'll show your hand. Don't waste time manufacturing a fever. Make several inexplicable trips to the bathroom and spend a considerable amount of time there. For added effect, feign some moans, but don't overdo it.

He was already at a disadvantage because everyone knew he didn't want to go duck hunting. Therefore, his symptoms would be suspicious no matter what. But if he spent enough time bellyaching, his father would eventually give up. It wasn't the most honorable thing Greyson had ever done—he understood that—but what choice did he have? If his parents ever actually listened to him, if they cared even one *iota* that he didn't want to traipse into the marsh at the break of dawn to watch his father kill ducks with a shotgun, if they had one *dollop* of interest in the things Greyson actually *wanted* to do, he wouldn't have to lower himself to faking illnesses.

But this is what it's come to, Greyson thought, at four in the morning during his fifth trip to the bathroom.

Ultimately, it was Trevor who saved the day.

"Just let him stay home, Dad," he'd said, from the other side of the bathroom door. "All he'll do is whine the whole time anyway."

So Greyson had stayed home "sick," which also meant he couldn't go to the football game in Saintlodge that afternoon. It was a worthy trade-off, in Greyson's opinion. He liked going to the games with Dorothy, but not as much as he hated the idea of duck hunting.

Greyson planned to go back to sleep after his father's truck roared off (with Zucchini inside, fidgeting with excitement, no doubt), but he was hopelessly awake. His mother was still sleeping; he hoped she wouldn't give him a hard time when she woke up.

He imagined a scenario that he knew would never

happen. His mother telling him that he didn't need to go hunting if he didn't want to, then asking him if there was something else he'd rather do instead, and him telling her that he wanted to help her make the pillows so he could feel the thrum of a machine under his fingertips. And then he would show her all the images he'd saved on his phone and ask if she knew how to make things like scarves and hats, and if so, could she teach him?

Outfits danced in his head now, right at this moment. He thought specifically about this black-and-white bespoke Chanel tweed suit that Kate had once worn. Greyson wondered how he could take that idea and turn it into something else. He imagined Kate standing next to him on the banks of Fawn Creek, both of them holding fishing rods. How could he change her clothing so it made sense in this scenario?

Greyson blinked at the ceiling as each element came into focus. For one thing, no one would ever want to wear tweed in south Louisiana. It would have to be a lighter fabric. And sleeveless, maybe, but still with the buttons down the front.

He sat up and reached under his bed. At the beginning of the school year, he'd planned to keep a journal, but he never actually felt like writing in it. The single-subject, spiral-bound notebook had languished in the same spot since August, gathering dust, all its pages blank.

Until now.

He sketched and sketched and sketched until he fell asleep again, notebook under his pillow. He slept until the afternoon, when his phone dinged him awake. A text from Dorothy.

Orchid is fraternizing with the enemy! it said.

❀ *25* ❀

Janie didn't usually spend Saturday nights by herself. On a normal weekend, Abby would spend the night or Janie would go to Renni's or Abby and Janie would go to Renni's together. But on *this* Saturday night, she wanted to be alone, in her room, earbuds tucked into her ears, playing music at full blast.

She was on her neatly made bed, listening to the saddest playlist she could find, when Madeline burst through the door without even knocking.

Madeline had all the typical traits of a little sister— she was annoying, asked a million questions without shutting up, and did things without asking. *And* she was spoiled. Janie had long suspected that her parents favored

Madeline. Coincidentally, Madeline felt the exact same way, only about Janie.

Madeline launched herself onto Janie's bed, where she landed with such force that one of the pillows fell on the floor.

"Ugh, Mee-Wee!" Janie said as loudly as possible, without looking up. She paused her music. "What do you want?"

Madeline shrugged. "Nothing."

Once upon a time, people called her "Maddy," but she'd recently insisted that she wanted to be known as "Madeline" because it sounded more sophisticated. Janie had her own name for her, though—Mee-Wee, because the day she came home from the hospital, she was so tiny that their father called her "little pee-wee." Janie couldn't say "pee-wee," though. Only "mee-wee."

"What're you doing?" Madeline said.

"Trying to find music." Scroll, scroll.

"Why are you in your pajamas? It's only six. Are you going to bed, or are you just plain lazy?"

"Neither." Janie looked at her sister. She'd drawn something on both cheeks, but it was hard to tell what it was. Flowers? Rainbows? Balloons? "What are you supposed to be?"

"I'm a girl who lives in the woods behind the school.

I wear a flower in my hair, just like the new girl. See?"
Madeline patted her tangled head of blond hair, realized
her flower was missing, leaned over the bed to retrieve
it from the floor, then tucked it behind her ear. A plastic
petunia without a stem. "See?"

The flower promptly fell out again.

"Did you take that from one of Mom's arrangements?"

"No," Madeline said quickly. "Maybe."

Janie went back to her phone. "You're gonna be in so
much trouble if she sees you."

"What's the new girl like? I heard she's a witch. A nice
witch."

"A witch!" Janie shook her head. "Don't believe
everything you hear."

"Well. If she's not a witch who lives in the woods, then
what is she?"

"What do you mean, what is she? She's a girl."

"Yeah, but no one knows where she came from. Not
even Aunt Kiki and she knows everything."

Janie snorted. "Aunt Kiki does *not* know everything.
She just likes to gossip."

"That woman is like a mockingbird, repeating
everything she hears to anyone who will listen." That's
what Janie's dad said once.

"Is she nice, though?" Madeline asked. "The new girl?"

Janie thought about what had happened at the football game. As soon as Renni and Abby realized she'd been talking to Orchid, they'd peppered her with questions. Janie had answered vaguely. But she *did* mention the invitation to the dance. Maybe she shouldn't have. She didn't like the way Renni's face lit up. *As if you'd actually want to go with them,* Renni said. *That's hysterical.*

"I guess she's nice," Janie said to her sister.

Janie wanted to go back to her depressing playlist. She wanted to bury herself under the covers and forget every word Renni had said. She wanted to wake up with a different face, a prettier face with a cute little nose.

"What do you mean?" Madeline said. "Either a person is nice, or they aren't."

"Some people are a little of both."

"Not in my opinion." That was one of her new favorite sayings. *Not in my opinion.* "You're either a nice person or you're not."

"When you're older, you'll know better."

"I know now. I don't need to wait until I'm older." She counted on her fingers: "I'm nice. Abby's nice. You're nice. Mom's nice. Aunt Kiki's nice. Dad is nice. My friend Ella—"

"Okay, I get it. Everyone you know is nice."

Madeline scrunched her nose. "Not everyone." She

paused. "And by the way, even though you're nice, you're also really annoying."

Janie lifted a pillow and lightly smacked her sister on the head. "Look who's talking!"

Madeline giggled. "So. Is the new girl nice? Yes or no?"

Janie sighed. "Yes. The new girl is nice."

"I knew it."

Madeline bounced off the bed. She was incapable of any delicate arrivals or departures. When she got to the door, Janie called her name and she didn't just turn around—she twirled.

Janie plucked the flower from where it had landed between the pillows.

"You forgot your flower, Mee-Wee," she said.

❀ *26* ❀

As much as Greyson didn't like being at his own house, he *really* disliked going to the Doucets. Dorothy's parents were nice enough, but the whole place felt like a museum. Even the temperature. Sixty-eight degrees on the dot. The surfaces were clean, practically sparkling, and the carpet looked like it had just been vacuumed five minutes earlier, no matter what. It was a small, sparse, meticulous house with earth-toned walls and muted furniture. No shoes strewn near the doorway or notebooks on the coffee table. No hoodies languishing or phone chargers tucked into sofa corners. No sewing room with bright, disorganized fabrics. The Doucet house shared much in common with Mr. and Mrs.

Doucet—understated, formal, and difficult to understand.

Much better, then, to spend time at Greyson's, where at least they could sit on the back patio and toss the tennis ball to Zucchini, like they were doing right now.

Dorothy—Didi—had just finished her recap of the previous day's football game. Not the actual game itself, of course, but the drama between Orchid and Renni and the enemy fraternizing that happened afterward.

"So Orchid didn't say *anything* when Renni made that comment about birds nesting in her hair?" Greyson asked. He wished Orchid had a phone so he could send her texts of solidarity, outlining all the reasons why Renni Dean was evil and should be ignored.

"No," Dorothy said. "She started to, though." Zuke bounded toward them and dropped the drool-soaked ball in Dorothy's lap. She tossed it for the millionth time. Zucchini went after it like a bullet, even though it hadn't gone very far. "She didn't seem very fazed."

"Renni Dean is an evil overlord and should be destroyed. I'm glad Orchid didn't let her get to her."

"I still can't believe she invited Janie to the dance after what they did. I mean, who does that?"

Zucchini returned. The smell of dog permeated the air.

"Sometimes she seems like she's almost *too* perfect, you know?" Greyson said.

"What do you mean?"

He shrugged. "She's just . . . like, she doesn't get upset about anything. She doesn't even seem upset that she's stuck in Yawn Creek."

Dorothy placed the grimy tennis ball on the cement and rolled it around absently with her index finger. Zucchini watched curiously, then sprawled down next to her. "Maybe she's just more mature than everyone else because she's lived all over the world. Maybe that's why she hangs out with us—because we're the only people with more than half a brain."

"Maybe." Greyson paused. "But . . . "

"But what?"

"I don't know. Her stories . . . they're like something out of the movies."

"If we ever got to go anywhere, we'd have better stories, too. But we're stuck here." Dorothy rolled the ball back and forth, back and forth. "Yesterday she told me a new one about her and Victor. It was kind of romantic."

Thank God Trevor was out with friends. If he heard Dorothy say that, Greyson would never hear the end of it. Trevor wasn't one for romance, even though he'd actually had girlfriends. It bewildered Greyson that any girl would willingly want to be Trevor's girlfriend, but such were the mysteries of the universe.

"She said she and Victor once ate éclairs under the Eiffel Tower," Dorothy continued. "She gave him a bite and he gave *her* a bite, and she got chocolate on her chin."

What had Orchid worn to this Eiffel Tower picnic? Greyson wondered. What about Victor? Did kids their age in Paris wear the same clothes as here? Considering most of Fawn Creek's wardrobe included camouflage, he guessed not. He imagined them sitting together, eating éclairs and wearing camo baseball caps. It was a strange image, but it *did* give him an idea. He could add camouflage to his collection—a collection that he had tentatively named "Paris Creek."

" . . . have you?"

Greyson blinked.

Uh-oh. Had Dorothy been talking this whole time?

"Have I what?" he said.

"Ever thought about it?"

"Ever thought about what?"

Dorothy sighed lightly, still rolling the tennis ball across the concrete. Even though they were in the shade, it was hot—as usual.

"Sorry, Didi," he said. "I wasn't listening. What were you saying?"

Dorothy picked up the tennis ball and stared at it. Her cheeks turned a light shade of pink. That was unusual.

She rarely experienced the red dread in front of him. Why would she? They were best friends. She could tell him anything.

"I was talking about Orchid's story," she said. "The one about her first kiss with Victor on the lock bridge."

"Oh."

"And I was just wondering . . . "—she took a deep breath—"if you ever thought about what you want *your* first kiss to be like?"

"Oh." Paris Creek faded away.

When he didn't answer immediately, she said, "Well?"

Greyson swallowed. "Not really."

"You haven't?"

"Well. Considering my options, no."

Dorothy frowned. "What do you mean, 'considering your options'?"

Greyson pictured his classmates, sitting at their desks. All ten of them. Eleven, if you counted Orchid. He couldn't fathom kissing *any* of them. Certainly not the Crawford or Kingery cousins. Gross. Colt, Max, or Daniel? No, thank you. The God Squad? They were nice and all, but . . . no way. And Orchid? Well, she was new and interesting and everything, but he had no desire to kiss her.

He explained this to Dorothy, then said, "There's no one in our class worth kissing."

She averted her eyes. "You forgot someone."

Greyson gazed out at the imaginary classroom again. Everyone was there.

"Who?" he said.

Dorothy paused. "Me."

Greyson almost laughed. Almost. The laugh was there—part nervousness, part amusement—and it nearly erupted out of his mouth, but in the moment just before it leaped into the air, he had the foresight to swallow it.

He didn't want to laugh at Dorothy, even if he meant nothing by it.

When Greyson's father had scolded him in front of the entire kindergarten because Greyson couldn't tie his own shoes, Dorothy had taken him into a corner and showed him how. *Over, under, pull it tight. Make a bow . . .*

Dorothy helped him with spelling when he couldn't put the letters together.

When he cut his knee in fifth grade, she hugged him and darted off to find a Band-Aid before he could even start crying.

He could never laugh at her, no. But the thought of them kissing felt all wrong. Despite all the years of teasing from Trevor—"Is that mousey Doucet girl your girlfriend or are you hers? Ha ha!"—he had never considered kissing her.

"I know we don't like each other that way," she added quietly. "But. I guess I'm just wondering . . . I mean . . . Do you think . . ." She swallowed. Her eyes were locked on the ball in her hand. "Will someone think I'm worth kissing someday?"

The red dread had crept its way up her neck now. He could see it, peeking above her T-shirt. He had been there when she got that T-shirt. His parents had taken them to the Pirate Festival in Lake Charles. They rode the Zipper so many times that he dreamed about it for two nights in a row. Before they left, Dorothy got a T-shirt that said "I Survived Pirate Fest."

His throat was suddenly dry. He studied her profile, but only for a second. Then he leaned over and kissed her cheek.

"That's just until you find your own Victor," he said. "And get your *real* first kiss."

The world around them quieted. She looked at him and smiled. He heard nothing but the steady, peaceful thumping of his heart. Just as he began to wonder what would happen next, she leaned over and kissed him back.

"You, too," she said.

WEEK TWO

❀ 27 ❀

Barnet Kingery's family had plenty of money, but you wouldn't know it by looking at him. If there was one thing Barn hated more than anything—more than school, even—it was clothes shopping. He flat-out refused to go anytime his mother tried to force him, and no amount of bribery would convince him. Over the summer she'd bought new clothes in the size she *thought* he wore. But that was three months ago, and he'd already grown. The camo shorts he was wearing today had been snug when she bought them and now they were just plain too small. He was getting taller, brawnier; she'd chosen shorts for the skinny little boy he'd been last year. The waistband dug into his skin and made it difficult to concentrate on Mrs. Ursu as she assigned new lab partners. He barely registered the sound of his own name when she paired him with Orchid.

Great. The new girl. He would have preferred anyone over the new girl.

It's not that he had an issue with her or anything; he just didn't want to make conversation. He knew everyone else in the class and they knew him. What did he have to say to this fancy big-city new girl? Nothing.

She smiled as she wandered over.

"Hello," she said.

He didn't reply.

Mrs. Ursu delivered a box of materials to each of their tables: a small container of water, a single penny, a bunch of worksheets (groan), and an old washcloth.

Whatever this was, Barn was not in the mood for it.

Orchid arranged the items neatly in front of them, but didn't say a word, thank God.

Barn fidgeted in his seat. He straightened his back, hoping to loosen the pinch on his waist. Ugh. He couldn't wait for this day to be over.

"The question we want to answer is, 'How many drops of water can fit on a penny?'" Mrs. Ursu said. She was standing in the front of the room with Abby. "One of you will serve as the conductor of the experiment. The other will document the findings."

Orchid turned to him.

"Would you like to document or conduct the experiment?" she asked.

Neither. He wanted to do neither. He wanted to do the least amount of work possible.

He shrugged. "Whatever."

"Well," Orchid said. "Do you have good handwriting?"

Ha. That was a joke. Barn had the opposite of good handwriting, partly because he didn't care and partly because he couldn't hold his pencil right. But really, who says there's one way to hold a pencil? He knew how to hold a rod and reel. He knew how to hold a hunting rifle. He knew how to hold his grandmother's hand at Sunday mass. What use did he have for holding pencils? No one did anything on paper, anyway.

Barn shook his head.

"My handwriting's pretty good, so I'll do the documentation and you can do the experiment." Orchid reached for the worksheets. "Do you have a pencil I can borrow?"

Ugh. Now he'd have to rummage through his backpack.

He leaned over to get the pencil—the stupid *godforsaken pencil*—and that's when it happened. All at once. Each stitch came loose in quick, unstoppable succession.

The back of his shorts ripped right down the middle.

Barn bolted upright. His face warmed.

Orchid looked at him. He looked at her.

How could he possibly do a science experiment like this? How could he stand up after class, much less walk around school? He needed to get to the office. He needed to call his mom.

He waited for Orchid to laugh. Janie would. Abby would. Anyone would. *He* would, if it had happened to someone else. Besides, Barn was good for a laugh anyway. He was clumsy, he knew that. In third grade he'd knocked over an entire display of books—they fell like dominoes—and kids laughed for days. In fifth grade he spilled Pepsi all over the cafeteria and Janie still reminded him about it.

How long would it take to live this down?

"Let's tell Mrs. Ursu you aren't feeling well," Orchid whispered. There wasn't a hint of amusement on her face. "Then you can go to the office."

The journey to the classroom door was a hundred miles. He'd have to walk by four tables.

"Don't worry," Orchid said. "I have a plan."

She leaned forward. Everyone else had started their experiment already. Greyson and Hallie were at the table in front of them, hunched over their penny. The back of Hallie's shirt said "*. . . then the buffet.*" What did that even mean? Some of these kids didn't make sense to him.

Especially Orchid, at this moment. He didn't know what she was thinking, but when she caught Greyson's attention, he assumed the worst. Greyson was her friend, wasn't he? And now she was going to tell him.

Great. Just great.

Barn didn't move. His embarrassment had made him immobile.

When Greyson turned around—and Hallie, by default—Orchid whispered, "Can we borrow your hoodie? I promise you'll get it back."

We?

Greyson's eyebrows knitted together. He looked like he was going to ask why. It was a sensible question, but Barn wished with every bone in his body that he wouldn't ask it.

Please don't ask.

Please don't ask.

"Sure, I guess," Greyson said. The hoodie was hanging on the back of his chair. He picked it up, passed it over, then went back to the experiment.

"I know it won't fit you," Orchid whispered to Barn. "But if you let it hang like this, it'll cover everything." She stood up, put her arms into it partway, and let it dangle down to her knees. Half on. Half off. "Leave it in the front office so Greyson can pick it up after class."

She handed him the hoodie.

He accepted it like a foreign object that he didn't know how to operate.

"Mrs. Ursu?" Orchid said, raising her hand. "Barn needs to go to the office. He isn't feeling well. I think he has a fever."

Barn was now wearing the hoodie. He let it hang as instructed.

Mrs. Ursu looked up from her penny. "Go ahead, Barn," she said. "Orchid, you can come up here with me and Abby."

Orchid and Barn lifted their bags at the same time, ready to relocate.

"Good luck," Orchid whispered, before sailing off to the front of the classroom.

Barn lumbered to the office without incident.

That's when he realized he'd only spoken one word to the new girl the entire time.

❀ ❀ ❀

Greyson + Hallie

"She gave Barn your hoodie," Hallie said after Barn left the classroom.

It was odd, Greyson had to admit. But he wasn't too worried. Orchid said he'd get it back, and he believed her. Besides, maybe she'd done him a favor. There was nothing interesting about a charcoal gray hoodie from the Old Navy in Lake Charles. He'd only bought it because he got cold at school sometimes. He'd rather cloak himself in something with more visual pizzazz. A floor-length flowered trench coat or something.

"I'm sure she has her reasons," he said.

Hallie steadied the water dropper over the penny. "Is it true she lives in the woods?"

"No," Greyson said, more defensively than he intended.

"Where does she live?"

"I don't know."

"If you don't know, that means she might live in the woods." Hallie squeezed a drop. The water coated Lincoln's face. "That's one drop, because I was closer this time. And I did it at an angle."

Greyson wrote. *One drop. Close distance. At an angle.*

"Isn't it weird that she lived in all these places and then she moved *here*?" Hallie said. "New York, Paris, Thailand, Iceland, *Germany*?"

At lunch that day Orchid had told them about the two weeks she'd spent in Berlin. There was once a wall there, she said, that separated the west from the east. People weren't allowed to cross it. Families were torn apart. Couples couldn't be together. They wrote messages to each other on the wall; Orchid read all of them, but the one she remembered most was "Ava—You are my air, my sky, my moon! I will be with you soon. I promise!" in red paint.

Lunch had morphed into something new since Orchid arrived. The handyman, Mr. O'Brien, had cut the grass and cleared the hallway. Had Orchid caused that? Did she ask them to clear the way? Did she tell the teachers that only seventh graders were allowed outside? Surely Orchid couldn't do all that. And yet, it was so. Like a miracle.

"Yeah, I guess," Greyson said.

Hallie dried off the penny with the washcloth and prepared the dropper for another test. Then she stood up. The front of her shirt said "Follow Me to Saintlodge Baptist Church."

"I'm going to do it from far away this time," she said. She raised the dropper above her head as high as she could.

"That's too far," Greyson said. "No way you'll be able to land on it."

"Watch me," said Hallie. She steadied her hand. "Behold my mad skills." She adjusted her aim, then lowered her voice. "I really like her and everything, but there's something she's not telling us."

She squeezed the dropper.

A dollop of water landed squarely on the penny.

"See?" she said. "Told you."

Colt + Daelyn

"I have a theory that her parents are, like, spies or something. I know it sounds stupid, but what other explanation could there be?" Daelyn said.

"About a million," said Colt, filling the dropper.

He did not want to talk about Orchid Mason. He had moved on from his stupid crush. Everyone said she already had a boyfriend—even if he did live in France or wherever—and besides, he didn't need to focus on one girl at the dance. If he took Orchid, then he wouldn't be able to talk to any of the other girls. Sure, she was pretty—though the more he looked at her, the more he thought she was just *okay*—but there would be lots of girls at the dance, some from Saintlodge. So what if Orchid told Abby she didn't like him? What did he care? Besides, she was weird. After the game on Saturday she'd come up to him, Max, and Daniel to tell them what a tremendous job they did. "Great catch in the third quarter, Max." "Amazing throw at the end, Colt!" "Good punt return, Daniel!" Then she just took off.

"That was random," Max had said.

"Yeah, and what did she mean 'good'?" Daniel said. "That punt return was *legendary*."

Anyway. Who does that, besides someone's *mom*?

"Name some, then," Daelyn said, tapping her pencil against the worksheet.

"Name some what?"

"Your theories on Orchid."

"I have no theories, because I don't care." He held the dropper directly over the penny. Squeezed and missed.

"You don't care," Daelyn said, though it wasn't clear if she was making a statement or asking a question. "I thought you liked her."

"What? Please." He re-aimed. "I don't like her. I was just being nice."

Missed again.

Daniel + Max

"I think I'm going to ask Hallie to the dance," Daniel said. He leaned his head back and squeezed two drops of water into his open mouth. "Yum. Tasty."

"Get serious," Max said.

"I *am* serious. It's tasty. I'm dying of thirst."

"You know what I mean."

Daniel refilled the dropper and scooted the penny closer.

Max nudged him. "Come on, seriously. Why Hallie? She's not even that pretty."

"Believe it or not, Max Bordelon," Daniel said, without looking up, "you are not the authority on good looks."

"If you say so."

"I say so," said Daniel. "Besides, I like Hallie. She's funny."

"So?"

"So. I'm funny. She's funny. We can get married and birth a hoard of stand-up comedians."

"Who says you're funny?"

"Me and the great God above." Daniel sat up. "Two drops that time." He tapped the paper in front of Max. "Document, my lowly assistant."

Max documented the data. "The dance sounds kinda dumb, if you ask me."

"I didn't."

"The three of us were supposed to go, man. A guy thing. If you go with Hallie, what then?"

Daniel shrugged. "You and Colt can still go. Or ask Janie. She likes you."

"Me and Colt can't go *by ourselves*. That'll look so—"

"You and Colt could ask Daelyn and Baylee. Then we can have a triple date."

Max scrunched up his nose. "No thank you. Pass. I have standards."

"Daelyn and Baylee have standards, too. If they're low enough, they might agree to go with the two of you."

"Ha ha."

Daniel squeezed another drop of water in his mouth.

"Told you I was funny," he said.

✿ ✿ ✿

Dorothy + Slowly

"Can you do me a favor?" Slowly asked.

Dorothy hadn't been thrilled to be paired with Slowly. He wasn't great at documentation and he wasn't great with the dropper. The edge of their paper was wet, and his handwriting was difficult to decipher. But she focused on the positive. She hadn't been paired with Janie.

"Sure," Dorothy said.

Slowly nodded toward the worksheet.

"You put my name as Slowly." He cleared his throat. "Do you mind erasing it and putting 'Lehigh'?"

Dorothy erased it, no questions asked. She was embarrassed, but not sure why. Everyone had called him Slowly for so long; she'd never given it a second thought.

"Sorry," she said, blowing the eraser dust away. She wrote *Lehigh*. "Isn't it interesting that you're getting rid of a nickname and using your real name, and I'm doing just the opposite?"

"What do you mean?"

"I'm trying to go by my new nickname now."

"What's your new nickname again? You probably told me, but I forgot."

Dorothy straightened up and said, "Didi."

Slowly didn't say anything for a moment. She

expected the worst. But then he just extended his hand and said, "Hi, Didi. I'm Lehigh. Pleased to make your acquaintance."

Dorothy laughed. "Pleased to make your acquaintance, Lehigh."

They shook hands, then got back to work.

Abby + Mrs. Ursu + Orchid

"How do you like Fawn Creek so far?" Mrs. Ursu asked.

Abby and Orchid stood on either side of her.

"It's not so bad," Orchid said.

Abby leaned forward. "It must be *so boring* compared to all the other places you've lived. I bet you're going crazy here. I hope you kept in touch with all your friends."

Orchid shrugged. "Every place is different."

"Well said." Mrs. Ursu slid the penny toward Orchid and handed her the dropper. "Each of you can take turns doing the experiment. I'll write the results." She picked up her pencil. "We're going to document how many drops will fit on this penny, and which variables come into play. For example, are we able to use more or fewer drops if we hold the dropper far away? What if we hold the dropper at an angle? It's easy to make assumptions, but you have to view things from all different sides."

Orchid filled the dropper. "You know what's interesting?

This place is called Fawn Creek, but I haven't seen a creek anywhere."

Abby lit up. "Really? The creek isn't far from here. Where do you live?"

"Pretty close," Orchid said. She delicately squeezed two drops onto the penny. Mrs. Ursu took notes.

"We should go after school," Abby said. "I can show you the way. Janie can come, too. Sometimes we go fishing there with our dads."

Mrs. Ursu frowned. "I'm not sure it's a good idea to fish in that creek. It runs right behind Gimmerton."

Abby was already texting under the table, saying, "What do you think, Orchid? Wanna go?"

The plans were half-made before Orchid even said yes.

Janie + Baylee

"*Everyone* at my church is talking about her," Baylee said.

"Why would anyone in Saintlodge care about a new girl here?" Janie asked. She was already bored with the conversation. And she was tired of talking about Orchid. Renni texted her daily for news about Colt and Orchid—news that didn't even exist, since nothing was going on.

I don't think he likes her, Janie texted last night.

Then WHY is he ignoring me?? Renni replied.

Janie could think of a hundred reasons. Her fingers itched to type them.

Talking to you can be exhausting because you never have anything good to say.

Maybe he doesn't trust you.

Maybe you make him feel bad for no reason.

But all she said was *Who knows.*

The stupid thing was, Renni didn't even seem to like Colt anymore—at least not in a like-like way. She talked about going to the dance with Ethan, that annoying blond kid with the skateboard who had said the kids from Fawn Creek were all related to each other.

Honestly, the more Janie thought about it, it was all so *boring.*

"People are saying that she's, like, too gorgeous to be believed," Baylee said. She lowered her voice as she wrote their names on the worksheets. "I heard that her hair is worth so much money, she had to get it insured."

Janie rolled her eyes. "What does that even *mean?*"

Baylee shrugged. "I don't know. That's just what I heard. And not from someone here. A seventh grader from Saintlodge asked me if it was true."

"That's ridiculous," Janie said. She casually touched her own hair. She'd always been proud of it. Thick, blond, long. "You have Barbie hair," Mee-Wee always said. But suddenly that seemed so predictable. Downright bland.

I'm an ugly girl with boring hair.

"I also heard some stuff about Renni," Baylee said.

Janie dropped her hand and perked up. She found herself hoping it was something terrible. A vicious rumor with teeth.

You're a horrible person, Janie Crawford. Why would you think that about your best friend?

"What stuff?" Janie asked.

Baylee tapped the stack of worksheets against the table to straighten them. *Tap, tap, tap.* "Just stuff. Nothing too bad, but . . . "

"But what?"

"Some girls at my church said she hangs out with sketchy kids. I don't know who they are or anything, but . . . they get in trouble a lot. Supposedly."

"What kind of trouble?"

"Pulling fire alarms. Getting in fights. That kind of stuff." Baylee moved the dropper in front of Janie, as if to say *Let's get started.* But Janie was not in the mood for science. It had been a few days since the football game, but she still wasn't over it. Everywhere she went she heard the words *horse horse horse.* She wondered if other kids said that about her, too. Was everyone thinking it?

"This girl at my church says they're a bunch of . . . "

Baylee cleared her throat. "Let's just say, 'mean people.' So I guess Renni should fit right in with them." As soon as the words left her mouth, Baylee's eyes widened in horror. "Don't tell her I said that."

Janie was about to reply when her phone buzzed. She peeked at the text under the table.

"Is that Renni?" Baylee whispered, her voice heavy with dread, as if Renni had heard everything.

"No," Janie replied. Really, Baylee was so *irritating* sometimes. "It's Abby. She wants to go to the creek with Orchid after school."

Janie sighed. Orchid this, Orchid that. Wasn't there *anything* interesting happening in Fawn Creek other than Orchid freaking Mason?

She glanced at the window, hoping that somehow she could climb through it.

The day had started sunny, but the sky was cloudy now.

Perhaps a storm was on its way.

❀ *28* ❀

A few hours later, there they were—Janie, Abby, and Orchid—turning off a worn footpath not far from the school and walking toward the creek from which the town got its name. Janie and Abby headed for a cluster of trees dripping with moss. Orchid followed.

Instead of sitting right away, Abby opened her arms ceremoniously and said, "This is Fawn Creek."

Orchid squinted out at the water and smiled. A light hum of noise filled the air. Buzzing mosquitoes. The plinks and splashes of unseen creatures. A faint trickle.

"It's nice," Orchid said. "Peaceful."

Janie was going to make a wisecrack, then realized she didn't have one. It *was* nice and peaceful. This was where her dad had taught her how to fish. This was where she'd played hide-and-seek as a little girl, usually with Abby, Barn, and Slowly. Barn was good at finding people, but terrible at hiding. Slowly always picked the same spots to hide. He got caught every time.

Orchid seemed strangely out of place here. Maybe because she was new, and Fawn Creek wasn't accustomed to anything unfamiliar. Maybe because her two sidekicks weren't with her. Janie wondered vaguely where Greyson and Dorothy were, but she didn't want to ask, because then it might look like she cared.

"What are we doing here, anyway?" Janie asked. There was a bite in her voice, though she wasn't sure why. Sometimes she was spiteful for no reason whatsoever.

"Janie's at that age," her mother said to Aunt Kiki often. What did that mean *exactly*? Janie never had the guts to ask.

Abby shrugged and sat down. "Just something to do. Orchid's never been here."

Orchid sat, too. She tucked her dress under her legs.

Janie looked at the sky full of clouds. *Okay sure, I'll sit, too,* she thought, but just as she was about to lower herself to the ground, she heard a series of high-pitched voices and giggles, which she recognized right away. "The God Squad's here," she said.

And sure enough, there they were.

"Where did they get the name 'God Squad'?" Orchid whispered.

She'd directed the question to Abby, but Janie answered—and not in a whisper—as Baylee, Hallie, and Daelyn joined them in the clearing.

"That's what they call themselves. The God Squad. Right, girls?"

Janie turned toward Orchid and said, "It's because they pray for our sins. We commit so many of them, we need three girls to pray for us."

Daelyn picked up a pebble and tossed it in their direction. "For your information, we're *proud* to call ourselves the God Squad."

Hallie shoved a piece of Big Red gum in her mouth. She didn't offer any to the rest of them. *Not very Christian-like,* Janie thought. If Jesus had gum, no doubt he'd offer every person a piece, even if it was Big Red, which was Janie's least favorite flavor, but whatever.

"You should come to church with us, Orchid," Hallie said. "Unless you go to the Catholic church in town like everyone else?"

"But even if you do, you can still visit ours," Baylee added. "We accept all faiths."

Come to think of it, Janie thought, *it wasn't very Christian-like for them to invite themselves to the creek, either.* Janie had told Baylee they were coming here, but she never said, *Hey, you and the other Jesus freaks should totally join us.*

"No thanks," Orchid said, waving her hand delicately. "Church isn't really my thing."

"I bet no one goes to church in Paris and New York," Abby said. "They probably do actual fun stuff."

"Church *is* fun," Daelyn said. "Our church is, anyway. We do this thing where we—"

"Ohmygod, no one *cares* about your church," Janie said. "If I had a choice between hearing about your church and writing five hundred poems for Mr. Agosto, I would literally start writing poetry right now."

Mr. Agosto had been on a poetry kick lately, much to their dismay. Yesterday he'd hinted that they'd have to write something called 'I Am' poems by the end of next week. Worse yet, the poems would be displayed for all to see. Wasn't this, like, an assignment for second graders? Couldn't teachers ever come up with original homework?

"Fine, Miss Whatever," Daelyn said.

"Anywaaaaay," Abby continued. She leaned forward, head tilted toward Orchid. "So what kinds of stuff did you do, besides *not* go to church?"

"She's already told us," Janie said. "She's probably

getting tired of telling us. Monkey beaches. Make-out sessions on bridges. Blah blah blah."

Orchid caught Janie's eye, then looked away and scanned the group, all sitting in a circle with her.

Janie was being a jerk. Janie *knew* she was being a jerk. She didn't quite know *why* she was being a jerk. Only that she was.

Maybe because she was tired of hearing about big-city this and that. And how beautiful Orchid was. And how she supposedly needed insurance for her hair.

"Well . . . " Orchid said. "There was this one game we liked to play."

"Oooo!" Abby's eyes were perfect curious circles. "What kind of game?"

"It's not like Truth or Dare, is it?" Daelyn asked. "I hate Truth or Dare."

Hallie blew a bubble. "That's because you're a chicken."

"It's not like Truth or Dare," Orchid said. "It's called Mirror Mirror. Do you want to play?"

The girls were quiet. So quiet. Janie knew what they were thinking. She saw it on their faces. They wanted to play, but they didn't want to play. No one wanted to be the coward. No one wanted to be the one who said, "Can you explain the rules first?" Each of them had the shared knowledge that games could be dangerous. Renni reminded them of that last year—right at this spot, actually, with this same group of people, except Orchid wasn't there, and Barn and Slowly were. Renni's truths and dares were too biting to be fun.

Barn, I dare you to be my servant for the rest of the afternoon. You have to ask for my permission to speak, and you have to do anything I say.

Slowly, who do you think is the ugliest girl in the circle? You have to be honest.

Baylee, I dare you to show us your bra.

The truths and dares went round and round and Janie had wished the whole time that Colt would show up with his friends because Renni was quieter when he was there. And all the while Janie laughed at everything because part of her worried what would happen if she stood up to Renni, told her to shut up, told her she was a jerk. The way Renni described things, she made it seem like her behavior was totally normal and everyone else was too sensitive or didn't have a good sense of humor. And then you'd think it over and decide, maybe she's right, maybe I *am* making a big deal out of nothing. Besides, if this was how Renni treated her friends, Janie certainly didn't want to be her enemy. It was an endless struggle trying to stay in Renni's good graces. But no one said friendship was easy, right?

Janie knew they were all thinking about that dreaded

game of Truth or Dare. Daelyn, for example. Renni had dared Daelyn to say the worst words she could think of because she knew Daelyn considered it sinful and immoral, and when Daelyn refused, Renni shouted a slew of swears at the top of her lungs and called Daelyn a prude. That's when the God Squad left—mumbled that they had to go home, the mosquitoes were eating them alive, and whatever other excuse they could think of—and the next day Renni told everyone she made Daelyn cry.

They might be afraid, but not me, Janie thought now. *I'm the queen of this circle.*

"Yes," Janie finally said. "We want to play. Don't we, girls?"

They all nodded hesitantly in succession. Yes. Yes. Yes. Yes.

Clouds swirled overhead.

"Okay," Orchid said, smiling that oh-so-perfect smile. Too gorgeous to be believed, supposedly. "Let's play."

❀ *29* ❀

I *didn't want to go, anyway,* Didi told herself as she nibbled the after-school snack her mother put out for her. She sat at the kitchen table, but wished she could be in her room, staring at the ceiling or talking to Greyson. But food wasn't allowed in her room and she never left her mother's snacks uneaten, even if she wasn't hungry. Even if it was something she didn't like, such as RITZ crackers with small blocks of cheddar cheese, which was what she was eating right now.

"How was school?" her mother asked as she flipped through the afternoon mail.

"Fine," said Didi. "How was your day?"

"Fine," said her mother.

Right on script as always.

But Didi didn't want to follow the script. She wanted to say, *My new friend Orchid asked me and Greyson if we wanted to go to the creek after school because she's meeting some kids over there—the Crawford girls, actually—and I kinda wanted to go, but only if Greyson went, but he didn't want to go so he said no thanks and I said no thanks too, because the thought of being around Janie and Abby makes me nervous and shaky and to be honest, I don't think Orchid should go either, but she makes her own choices, and now I'm here and they're at the creek and what if they tell Orchid something bad about me, like that I have boils or something, and she decides not to be my friend anymore?*

"Mom?" Didi said. The cheese felt like a boulder in her throat.

"Yes?"

Have you ever felt awkward? Have you ever felt like you never know what to say?

Didi picked up the last cracker on her plate.

"Thank you for the snack," she said.

I am an actress.

Metaphor.

❀ 30 ❀

Greyson was thinking about the subway.

He'd never ridden a subway. He'd never ridden any form of public transportation in his whole life. He'd never even been outside of Louisiana, unless you count weekends to Sea World in Texas.

When people peppered Orchid with questions at lunch—"What kind of food did you eat in Thailand?" "How tall is the Eiffel Tower?" "What kind of music do the kids listen to over there?" "What do they watch on TV?" "Could you understand what people were saying?" "Do they really drive on the wrong side of the road?"—Greyson had an entirely different set of curiosities. He wanted to know what New York City smelled like. How the hot dogs tasted when you bought them from those carts. The right way to hail a cab. (Are you supposed to whistle? What if you don't know how?) He wanted to know if there was traffic at one a.m. in the morning, and what it was like to stand in the crown of the Statue of Liberty, and what the draping of her gown looked like up close.

So that afternoon, just before Orchid had invited them to the creek with Janie and Abby (*That's a big no thank you,* Greyson had thought), and right after he got his hoodie from the office, he'd asked her: "What's it like to ride on the subway?"

Orchid hesitated. Then she said, "Rumbly."

"And?"

"Crowded."

Greyson wanted more. He wanted what Mr. Agosto called "sensory details." But Orchid seemed uninterested in providing them. Maybe she was tired of answering questions. Maybe that's why she changed the subject to the creek.

But that didn't stop Greyson from thinking about the subway as he sat in the corner of his mother's sewing room. He pulled up YouTube videos. He'd seen the subway before, of course, on TV and stuff, but he'd never wondered much about it before. This time, though, he watched clips of real people, not actors, going about their daily lives in New York. Here was a man in a cable-knit sweater. Here was a woman with a poofy Afro. Here was a dog on a skateboard. Here was a woman in a miniskirt, dancing. Here was a person with long, pink fingernails and a necktie. Here was an old woman in a wedding dress. An old man with a stuffed animal. There were people wearing burkas and turbans and saris and ball gowns and ripped jeans and dreadlocks and pajamas. They all crowded together, on the same seat. Clutching the same pole. Everyone was different, but they were on the same train. It was so far away from Fawn Creek, it might as well be on another planet. In Fawn Creek he'd see Janie's mom behind the counter at the restaurant. Barn's dad selling tackle. Trucks rumbling toward Gimmerton. The same people. Same faces. Same routines. Day after day.

But it was possible to get out of here, wasn't it? New York wasn't billions of light years away. New York was here, on this mass of land, in the United States of America. It was reachable. Orchid was proof.

He pictured himself on the subway, next to the person with the pink fingernails. But not him as he was now. A better version of him. Another Greyson, one who never wore boring clothes and always looked like he had somewhere important to go.

Real life had a way of pulling you back from your

dreams, though. Like right now, there were two knocks on the door, and Trevor stuck his head in without waiting for Greyson to say anything.

What was the point of knocking if you were just going to barge in?

"Hey, *Gayson,*" Trevor said, his dumb head wedged between the door and the frame. "Mom said it's your turn to mow the backyard, so stop sewing pillows and get out there before it rains." He left the door open and disappeared down the hall.

There were only twenty seconds left of the video Greyson was watching, but he got up and closed the door anyway. It was only twenty seconds, but they were his.

❀ *31* ❀

Janie walked through her front door moments before the quiet rain burst into a thunderstorm. It was as if the weather had waited for her to make it safely home and despite her crappy week, terrible mood, and that word bouncing around in her head (*horse horse horsehorsehorse*), she felt like she just might be the kind of girl capable of controlling the weather.

She breezed a quick hello to her aunt Kiki, who was on the couch in the family room, then rushed to her bedroom, took off her shoes, and went to the window to watch the rain with her feet pressed into the plush carpet. She wondered if the other girls made it home before getting drenched. Abby and Janie lived closest to the creek, but the God Squad lived near the trailer park. And Orchid . . . well, who knew where she lived?

There was a crash of thunder, followed by the unmistakable patter of Mee-Wee's feet charging down the hall. Her little sister flung open the door.

"We were wondering when you'd get home," Mee-Wee said. "Aunt Kiki is here."

"I know," Janie said. "I saw her when I came in."

Their aunt was watching one of her medical dramas. Janie could hear the muffled sounds of a fictional emergency downstairs.

"Mom was going to make us go to the restaurant, but she says we don't have to now because of the rain," Mee-Wee said.

Thank God. Janie was in no mood to serve jambalaya and pistolettes. She wanted to stay right here, at this window, forever and ever, feeling just as she did now.

Mee-Wee threw herself across Janie's bed.

"Why are you staring out the window?" she asked.

"Just thinking."

"About what?"

"Stuff."

"What kind of stuff."

"Just stuff."

"Boys?"

"No."

"School?"

"No."

"What, then?"

Janie sighed. She was about to ask Mee-Wee to leave—*I want to be alone and watch the thunderstorm and just have a moment to replay the afternoon*—but she surprised herself by moving away from the window and joining her sister on the bed.

"I was thinking about a game I played this afternoon," Janie said.

Mee-Wee's face lit up. She hadn't yet learned how dangerous games could be.

"What kind of game?" she asked.

"It's called Mirror Mirror."

"How do you play?" Mee-Wee was sitting up now, straight as a telephone pole, with her legs tucked underneath her.

Janie recited Orchid's words as best as she remembered them. "Before you play Mirror Mirror, you have to take an oath of loyalty and secrecy to everyone in the circle."

Mee-Wee looked around. "We're not in a circle."

"We can still take the oath. It goes like this." Janie paused. "I solemnly swear that the information revealed here will not leave the confines of this circle—er, bed."

"I solemnly swear that the information revealed here will not . . . Wait, what was it again?"

"Will not leave the confines of this bed."

" . . . will not leave the confines of this bed," Mee-Wee said. "Okay. Now what?"

"Now you have to tell me something mean someone has said about you in the past. Something that really hurt your feelings."

Something that you can't stop thinking about, Orchid had said. *Something that sliced you in two. Even if you think it's stupid. Something that you think about when you look in the mirror.*

Mee-Wee frowned. "I don't like thinking about mean stuff people have said to me."

"Of course not. Who does? But that doesn't mean we don't think about it. Right?"

Sometimes it's better to share it with someone else. I can go first, if you want. When no one said anything, Orchid had continued. *Just recently, someone made a hurtful comment about my hair. They made a joke about birds nesting there.* She looked around. *Who wants to go next?*

"I guess," Mee-Wee said. She looked down. "Simon Landry said I smell like a catfish, because we own a seafood restaurant."

Simon Landry was Daniel Landry's little brother.

Simon had a crop of red hair, like Daniel, and a face full of freckles.

Mee-Wee looked up. "Is that the end of the game? Because that wasn't very fun."

"No," Janie said. "Next is the best part."

"What? We go to Simon's house and beat him up?"

"No. Now's the part where I tell you all the *greatest* things about yourself," Janie said. "So when you think about what Simon said, you'll remember all this stuff, too."

"Okay."

Janie looked directly at her sister. *It's good to look people in the eye when you tell them something you want them to remember,* Orchid had said.

"Madeline Crawford," Janie began. "I think you have the most amazing smile in the world. It could light up the whole neighborhood!"

As if on cue, Mee-Wee smiled bright.

Janie had wanted to smile, too, when the girls went around the circle at the creek. But something stopped her. She didn't want them to know that she was listening; that she cared about their compliments. Why was that? What was so bad about them knowing that she cared? When the God Squad did their rounds, all of them hugged afterward. But Janie's expression never wavered. She wasn't *rude* or anything. She said thank you to all of them. But she didn't reach out for hugs. Her eyes didn't fill with tears the way Daelyn's did when all of them—yes, even Janie—gave her an honest appraisal of all her gifts.

You never have anything bad to say about anyone, Orchid had said to Daelyn. *I noticed that right away.* The others mentioned how loyal Daelyn was, how you could trust her with your life, how dedicated she was to the things she believed in. Janie mentioned how Daelyn used to help Slowly with his homework, and Janie always thought it was nice of her to take time to do that.

Then it was Hallie's turn. *Someone once called me trailer trash because I live in Fox Run.* Afterward, they all told her how funny she was. What a great sense of humor she had. How she made people smile. How she was *so* smart. How she wore the best T-shirts.

"Also . . . ," Janie continued, to Mee-Wee. "You make me laugh just about every day. And even though you come into my room without asking, I'm always happy to see you."

Mee-Wee raised her eyebrows.

"Okay, not always," Janie said. "But most of the time. Things are happier when you're around. You're like a little ball of bright energy, filling up the space."

Mee-Wee spread her arms and wiggled her fingers, as if reverberating joy directly out of her fingertips. "What's the next part?" she asked.

"That's it for today," Janie said.

"That's not a very long game."

"Well, it moves fast when there's only two of you."

In the circle that afternoon, there had been six of them.

When it had been Janie's turn to share something that sliced her in two, she thought of that word (*horsehorsehorse*) and Max, but she couldn't bring herself to say it. She felt warm and shameful when she thought of it herself—how could she possibly share it with this circle of girls, all looking at her?

She picked something else instead.

"I used to sing," she had said. She cleared her throat. "Not, like, professionally or anything. Just to myself. In the shower, or just walking around, or while helping at the restaurant or whatever." She shrugged. "Then one day someone told me that I was embarrassing myself because I sounded like a dying animal."

She laughed lightly, expecting that they'd laugh, too. But they didn't.

Instead, they started their rounds.

I think you're the prettiest girl in school.

You have a great laugh.

I wish I had your hair.

On and on and on.

Now, less than an hour later, as she sat on the bed with her little sister, Janie felt light and happy. She replayed each compliment again and again, like a never-ending loop.

"That's a good game," Mee-Wee said, nodding approvingly.

Janie smiled. "I agree."

When the rain quieted, Mee-Wee went back to her room and Janie returned to the window. The world outside was wet.

She realized then that no one had complimented Orchid. The rain had started before they could.

She realized something else, too. All of their confessions started the same: "Someone once said" or "Someone told me." And in every instance—though no one said it aloud—that someone was Renni.

❀ *32* ❀

Didi worried that Orchid would find a place with the Crawford cousins and abandon her and Greyson, but that didn't happen. Orchid was the same Orchid, even after hanging out with Janie and Abby. By the time they all sat down for Mr. Agosto's class on Friday, Didi felt silly for even thinking it. Instead, she focused on Mr. Agosto as he talked about poetry. As usual, he was more excited than anyone else in the room at the prospect of discussing, studying, and—groan—*writing* poetry.

Not that Didi objected to poetry. She didn't even mind the idea of writing it. But Mr. Agosto had announced that some of their poems would be shared with the class. The thought of putting herself out there for all to see was enough to cause a year's worth of red dread.

"Does anyone know who Mary Oliver is?" Mr. Agosto asked, his eyes skimming across the thirteen of them.

Baylee raised her hand. "Isn't she the sophomore who moved to Texas last year?"

"No, goober," Hallie said. "That was Marianne Hollinger."

Mr. Agosto cleared his throat. "Mary Oliver was an American poet who won the National Book Award and the Pulitzer Prize," he explained. "One of her most famous poems is called 'Wild Geese.'"

He projected the poem on the board. Didi shrunk down in her seat. When Mr. Agosto projected things on the board, he usually called on someone to read it aloud.

Thankfully, he pointed at Daniel.

"Daniel, would you like to read the poem aloud, please?" Mr. Agosto said.

Daniel raised his eyebrows. "Would I *like* to? Or will I?"

Quiet laughter sailed through the room, but Mr. Agosto was unamused.

"Daniel, read the poem aloud," he said flatly. "Please."

Daniel sat up and sighed. He read with the least amount of enthusiasm possible, but it didn't matter to Didi because she focused on the words, not on Daniel's voice. These words especially:

Whoever you are, no matter how lonely,
The world offers itself to your imagination.

Didi, still slouched down in her seat, felt warm and embarrassed, as if Mary Oliver had written about Didi's private thoughts. Daniel read the poem so casually, his voice so uninterested. How did he do that? Didn't he feel every syllable, like she did?

She glanced around the room, examining her classmates, wondering how the poem made each of *them* feel. Baylee yawned. Hallie was secretly texting under her desk. Same with Janie and Abby. Barn and Slowly both looked half-asleep. The others wore blank expressions, from what she could tell.

She wished she could see Greyson, but all she had was the back of his head.

She didn't have a good angle on Orchid, either.

Didi tucked her hands in her lap and leaned forward. She repeated the lines to herself again and again.

Whoever you are, no matter how lonely,
The world offers itself to your imagination.

WEEK THREE

❁ 33 ❁

On Saturday Greyson woke up with a singular thought: *We need to find out where Orchid lives.* He couldn't say why, exactly, the idea hammered through his brain. Why did it matter? Maybe she lived in a big, two-story house like the Crawfords or Kingerys. Maybe she lived in a trailer like the God Squad. Maybe she lived in a hovel deep underground. It didn't matter to him where or how she lived—he just wanted to know where it was. Orchid was a puzzle of endless mystery and he wanted to solve it.

He reached for his phone. It was 10:10 in the morning. His family was already up; he could hear them. They were early risers. Just another way he was different from them.

He texted Dorothy—Didi—his plan.

Let's go into the woods behind the school and see if we can find Orchid's house.

There was no response and Greyson imagined Didi sitting there, staring at her phone, wondering if his idea was good or not, morally speaking. He knew what she was thinking. Would this violate Orchid's privacy? Why did it matter where she lived? Shouldn't they just wait until Orchid told them herself or invited them over?

He heard the front door open. The sounds of his father and brother leaving the house. Running errands together, no doubt. Greyson couldn't imagine willingly going with his father to King's or to the sporting goods store in Saintlodge, but Trevor was always at the ready, especially if it meant he could practice his driving.

His father's pickup truck rumbled to life and drifted away.

Maybe I'll just stay home and work on my sketches, Greyson thought.

But then his phone chimed with a text from Dorothy.

OK, it said.

❀ *34* ❀

Does this violate Orchid's privacy?, Didi thought, as she pulled on her sneakers. She hadn't done anything yet, but she already felt guilty. She was curious, though. She couldn't help herself. She wanted to know what Orchid's world looked like away from school. She wanted to put Orchid's life under a microscope, study it, and learn something, like how to exist without needing to hide all the time.

It was plain old nosiness, wasn't it? Sticking their noses where they didn't belong?

Shouldn't they just wait for Orchid to invite them over?

But by the time she wandered up to the Broussards' front porch—waving at Zucchini, who was at the fence wagging her tail—she was ready for adventure.

She was pleased to see that Mr. Broussard's truck was gone, which probably meant Trevor wasn't home, either. An added bonus.

Greyson's mother opened the door before Didi had a chance to knock.

"Saw you through the window," she explained, smiling. "Greyson's in the sewing room."

"Thanks," Didi said. She'd always liked Greyson's mom. Over the summer she'd given Didi an unused tube of lipstick ("Not my color," Mrs. Broussard said), and for days Didi put it on in the secrecy of her room. The Doucets did not allow her to wear makeup. Not until you're sixteen, they'd said. Didi wasn't sure what was so magical about sixteen that made lipstick permissible, but she didn't ask. She just agreed and carried on. As usual.

When Didi walked into the sewing room, she expected to see Greyson on the floor, scrolling through his phone, but instead he was standing in front of the full-length mirror holding pieces of fabric up to his chest. One swatch was red plaid. The other, purple.

Didi avoided her reflection in the mirror. She sat in Mrs. Broussard's sewing chair and swiveled back and forth.

"I like the purple one," she said.

"It's 'mulberry' actually," Greyson said.

Didi shrugged. "Looks like purple."

"Do you know how many colors fall under the purple umbrella? There's eggplant, lilac, periwinkle, violet—"

"Okay, I like the *mulberry*, then." Swivel, swivel. "What are you doing, anyway?"

Greyson tossed the swatches aside. "I'll tell you if you promise not to laugh."

Didi raised her eyebrows. Duh. When did they ever laugh at each other when it came to important things?

Greyson tapped the cover of his notebook, which sat next to the sewing machine. He'd been drawing in it endlessly for days and days, though he never showed Didi what he was doing. She figured he would, eventually.

"I'm thinking about doing something really stupid . . . I mean, I'm *considering* it," he said. "It's *potentially* stupid, I don't know . . . Maybe."

Didi stopped swiveling. "Let me guess. You're going to rob a bank and escape to France. All your plans are inside this notebook, and you need me to guard it with my life."

"Ha ha. Very funny," he said. "But no." He glanced at the door, as if Trevor would burst in any moment, even though they both knew he wasn't home. "Maybe even stupider than robbing a bank." He took a deep breath. "I want to design my own outfit—"

Didi stood up and clapped. "That's amazing! Why would that be stupid?"

"Because I want to wear it to the dance."

Didi stopped clapping. Her chest warmed. A dozen images immediately marched through her head, and all of them involved people laughing, pointing, or worse.

"Oh," Didi said.

She *wanted* to be supportive.

She *wanted* to say *great idea! Be yourself! Do your thing!* But originality didn't always seem like a good thing. Not here in Fawn Creek, anyway. Plus—she'd heard Renni Dean would be at the dance. This was just the kind of thing she'd love.

She searched her mind for a correct response but couldn't find one. What if his outfit came out all wrong and everyone made fun of him? Even if it *didn't* come out all wrong, people would make fun of him.

Greyson frowned. "Told you it was a stupid idea."

"No, it's not that," Didi said. She sat down again. "I think it's amazing you want to design your own outfit. I just . . . " She swallowed. The red dread inched up her neck. She decided to go with the truth. "I just don't want people to make fun of you. That's all." She sighed. "But if you want to do it, I'm in. One hundred percent. I don't know anything about how to make clothes, but I'll help if you show me what to do."

"Well, that's the thing," he said. "I don't know how, either."

"Then how are you going to make an outfit?"

"I have no idea," Greyson said.

"Maybe Orchid can help," Didi said.

"Maybe," Greyson said. He nodded toward the door. "So let's go find her."

❀ *35* ❀

By the time they reached the school, Greyson's shirt was plastered to his back. Dorothy had her hair tied into a messy ponytail. She didn't do that often—she hated to have her face on full display—but if it was hot or humid enough, and if there was no one else around, she'd gather it all together and secure it with a rubber band. Greyson loved when she wore it that way. Not because he liked her or anything. He just liked the thought that she was comfortable being with him the same way he was with her. Even if every person at the dance laughed at him, he knew she wouldn't. And that counted for something.

He had a rough sketch of his outfit in his notebook. Bright. Asymmetrical. Loud. The opposite of boring. He was so lost in the imaginary pockets and layers that he didn't realize Dorothy was talking. Luckily, he was able to get the drift easily.

" . . . and then what will we say if we *do* find her?"

"We'll just tell the truth," Greyson said. "We'll tell her we wanted to hang out and we wanted her help, so we came here to see if we could find her."

The school looked strange on the weekend. Like it was a different place. Lights out, empty parking lot, no one around. They stood on the sidewalk about a half block away, near the crosswalk where Orchid usually walked into the field and disappeared.

"It's like the school's asleep," Dorothy said.

Greyson smiled. It was uncanny how best friends could share the same thoughts sometimes.

"Is that a metaphor or a simile?" he asked.

"Simile."

They were side by side, almost shoulder to shoulder, with their backs to the street and their eyes forward, studying the vast field ahead, which stretched to a dense thicket of trees. Beyond that, the industrial towers of Gimmerton Chemical reached into the sky and blew white smoke into the atmosphere.

"Everyone's saying she's in witness protection," Greyson said.

"Some people say she lives in a treehouse," Dorothy added.

Greyson imagined Orchid leaning delicately against a tree trunk, wearing a white dress, like Emily Dickinson. "Maybe she does."

"There aren't any neighborhoods over there. We both know that. Nothing but Gimmerton."

"What if she's homeless or something?" Greyson said.

"No way."

"Well. It's just as likely as her living in a treehouse, isn't it?"

They didn't say a word as they made their way across the field, not until they reached the trees and saw something familiar sprouting from the ground. A white flower. Didi plucked it and tucked it behind her ear. It wouldn't stay put, though.

"How does she manage it?" Didi asked, slipping it into her buttonhole instead.

"I have a feeling we'll be able to ask her soon. Look." Greyson pointed to a newly worn trail through the trees. They froze simultaneously, as if waiting for the other person to take the first step.

Greyson felt like a character out of a fairy tale, about to charge into a dark forest. Only it wasn't dark, and it wasn't a forest. Not really. And he was pretty sure there was no humidity in the fairy tales. No cotton shirts clinging to sweaty skin.

Besides, nothing magical ever happened in Fawn Creek.

❀ 36 ❀

It wasn't a very long trail.

They'd only walked for a few minutes—long enough for Didi to silently recite the Mary Oliver poem in her head four times—when a clearing opened ahead.

No grass. Only overturned dirt. It was obvious that the trees had been cut down recently. And just ahead, a neighborhood. Well, sort of. Not exactly. *Would I call it a neighborhood?* Didi thought. There were no paved roads, but there were houses—nine of them—alongside rows of campers and RVs. The houses were identical. Small. No garages or driveways or backyards. And they were all on slats, but they weren't trailers. It looked as if someone had created a neighborhood in a hurry and delivered it here.

The entrance to the compound was protected by a gate. There weren't any cars, just trucks and SUVs, all coated with dirt.

"What is this?" Didi asked.

Neither of them moved.

"Don't know," answered Greyson.

One of the trucks had "BILDNER" emblazoned on the side. "What's 'Bildner'?" asked Didi.

"Don't know."

"What should we do?"

"Don't know."

Didi eyed the gate. "What if this is, like, some kind of restricted area, like in the movies?"

"If it is, then they aren't doing a very good job, since we're standing right here."

"I feel weird," Didi said. She looked down and realized that the white flower had fallen out of her buttonhole somehow. "Maybe we should just—"

A twig snapped nearby. Then, "Hey."

Orchid. She'd come up behind them like a butterfly.

Didi's heart plummeted. Her faced turned the brightest shade of red. She suddenly felt the need to apologize.

"Oh, hi, Orchid," Didi stammered. "I'm sorry. We just. I mean—"

"We wanted to see what you were up to today," Greyson said. "We thought you might want to hang out, if you're not busy. We would've texted you, but . . . " He shrugged.

Orchid smiled faintly. She seemed different here, away from school. She was wearing a faded T-shirt and an old pair of cargo pants with a drawstring. Her hair was in a lopsided ponytail. She seemed . . . dimmed, somehow.

Didi breathed in deeply, willing her heart to slow down.

"That's nice," Orchid said, not unkindly. She motioned to the trees behind them. "I was just walking around. I go for walks sometimes, in the woods. Kinda . . . searching for stuff, I guess."

"What kind of stuff?" Didi asked.

Orchid reached into her pocket and pulled out a small rock, the size of an egg. There wasn't anything remarkable about it, at least at first glance. But when she turned it over, a cluster of crystals—very small—glinted back at them.

"That's cool," said Greyson.

Didi nodded. "Yeah. Really pretty."

"I guess it's kinda childish, searching the woods for hidden treasures," Orchid said, slipping it back into her pocket. "But you never know what you'll find. I found an arrowhead once, when we lived in Baytown."

"Baytown," Greyson repeated. "Where's that?"

A part of Didi—the small, hopeful part that beat deep in her chest—thought Orchid would name a magical place, like Fiji or Taiwan or Morocco.

But Orchid said, "Texas," which was right next door.

✿ *37* ✿

"Is this where you live?" Greyson asked, motioning toward the collection of homes, campers, and RVs.

"Yeah." Orchid glanced at all of it as if she'd forgotten it was there. "Do you want to come over? I guess my dad won't mind."

"Sure," Greyson said. He exchanged looks with Dorothy as they followed Orchid past the fence into the compound. The expression on Dorothy's face was difficult to read. Furrowed eyebrows, flat-lined mouth. Like she was trying to solve a math problem.

"Mine is the one with the red truck in front," Orchid called, over her shoulder.

Greyson lifted his voice. "What is this place, anyway?"

They were nearing the house with the red truck. Because there were no paved roads or driveways, it was parked diagonally in front, not far from the small porch, where a large man leaned against the railing. He was eating an apple. His hands were huge. Big, thick hands that reminded Greyson of his father. He wore steel-toed boots, blue jeans, and a T-shirt with "Bildner Construction" on it.

"Hey, Dad," Orchid said. "These are my friends from school."

Her father straightened up and tossed the apple. It sailed beyond the truck and landed in the dirt. He swiped his palm against his jeans, then extended his hand as if they were all adults.

"Hi, friends from school," he said.

Greyson hadn't shaken many hands in his life, but his dad always said you could tell a lot by a handshake. "Real men don't have limp wrists," his dad had told him, more than once.

Greyson made sure to grip this man's hand with all his might.

"Strong handshake, son," Orchid's father said, nodding approvingly.

Greyson swelled with pride, though he tried not to show it.

Orchid's father lit a cigarette as the three of them went inside.

The house was sparsely furnished. As if they had just arrived, but already planned to leave. It smelled like fresh paint.

"This is a temporary camp for Bildner," Orchid said.

"What's Bildner?" Greyson asked.

"They do construction for places like Gimmerton. Like if they have a short-term project or whatever," Orchid answered.

Her room looked like a different universe from the rest of the house. Fairy lights dangled from the ceiling. There were flowers on the nightstand. Fake flowers, Greyson could tell, but bright and cheerful. Her bed was decorated with sunflower-shaped pillows and a bright yellow bedspread. A small bookcase was pushed in a corner with books neatly lined up on each shelf. Greyson recognized several titles, though he hadn't read any of them. *A Wrinkle in Time. Hurricane Child. The Secret Garden. A Wish in the Dark.* He'd never seen Orchid with a book. When did she read all these?

Above the bookshelf was a huge corkboard covered with photos. Greyson and Dorothy stood side by side, looking at it, as if they were conducting one of Mrs. Ursu's scientific investigations and all the answers would be found here. But no. There were only more questions. Why did she have so many photos of old signs? "Welcome to Baytown." "Welcome to Codgeville." "Welcome to Ferrisville." "Eagleton Welcomes You." And landscapes—trees, wildflowers, abandoned buildings, old 1950s burger shops.

No Eiffel Tower.

No Empire State Building.

No romantic bridges.

No monkey beaches.

No friends, even.

Greyson caught Dorothy's eye and held it until she looked away and pointed to one of the few photos with people in it. A woman with her arm around Orchid's shoulder. Orchid was round cheeked and wearing a romper.

"Is that your mom?" Dorothy asked.

Orchid was cross-legged on her bed, watching them. "Yeah," she said.

Silence filled every corner of the room until Greyson said, "Where is she?"

Orchid picked at a loose thread on her bedspread. "Around."

"Why do you have so many pictures of old signs and stuff?" Greyson asked. "How come there aren't any pictures of . . . "

His question drifted away.

Orchid laughed nervously. "Just stupid kid stuff, I guess. I like old signs. When you've lived in so many different places, you have to search for things that are . . . " She paused.

"That are what?" Greyson asked.

"Unique."

"How come there aren't any pictures of Paris or New York?" Greyson glanced at Dorothy. "Or Victor? Or any of the places you told us about?"

Orchid pulled, pulled at the thread. She looked down.

Greyson couldn't see her face, but ticks of silence slid by—*tick, tick, tick*—and he heard a sniffle. A light, quiet sniffle. The kind you make when you're crying, but don't want anyone to hear you.

When she raised her head, her eyes sparkled. A tear dangled on the tip of her nose.

"I just wanted to be someone different," she said. "Someone who went places."

Dorothy looked at Greyson, then glanced toward the corkboard. "But you *have* gone places," she said. She rattled off the names on the signs. "Baytown. Codgeville. Ferrisville."

"Those are all places like this," Orchid said. She pulled a tissue from a box on her nightstand and blew her nose.

"Small towns. Like this one. My father and I drop in and leave when the job is over. One town after another. And they're all the same."

Greyson frowned.

"What do you mean, they're all the same?" he asked.

"Every town. Every school. There's never anything to do. Everyone knows everyone. There's always a Renni, making people feel bad about themselves. There's always a kid like Slowly, who everyone treats like a dummy. There's always a Janie, who thinks she's better than everyone. There are always jocks, like Colt and his friends. There are always nice do-gooders, like the God Squad. And I'm always the new girl with old clothes and no phone and no mother." She took a deep breath and added quietly, "It's the same everywhere."

Greyson crossed his arms. Sure, Fawn Creek wasn't Paris. But it wasn't Codgeville or whatever, either.

"What are we, then?" he asked.

Orchid's eyebrows furrowed. "What do you mean?"

"You said there's always a Renni. There's always a Janie. So I assume there's always a Greyson and Dorothy." He moved a finger between him and Dorothy. "Which neat little box are we in?"

"Greyson," Dorothy said. "I don't think she meant—"

"I *know* what she meant," Greyson said. He narrowed

his eyes at Orchid. "Fawn Creek isn't original enough for you? Well, guess what. *You're* not original enough for Fawn Creek." He motioned toward the corkboard. "Obviously."

Orchid frowned. She looked pitiful, but the seed had cracked open in Greyson's chest and grown into full-fledged anger. How would Orchid describe *him* in the next small town she went to?

There's always a Greyson. The one who _____.

"I'm leaving," he said. He gestured to Dorothy on his way out. "Come on, Dorothy."

But Dorothy did not move.

She looked at Orchid.

She looked at Greyson.

"Are you coming or what?" Greyson said.

Dorothy walked to the bed and sat down. "I think I'll stay," she said quietly.

Greyson's heart squeezed into a tiny ball and pushed its way into his throat. "Fine, stay here and listen to more fairy tales," he said. "See you later, *Didi*."

❦ 38 ❦

The room was quiet after Greyson left.

Orchid looked at her lap. "Nothing I said came out right."

Didi didn't know what to say. She never did. Not really.

"I think he's just upset . . ." Didi began. She intended to say *I think he's just upset that you lied,* but that sounded too harsh and accusatory, and she didn't want to be harsh and accusatory. She decided to let the sentence end right there. Even though it was true. Even though Orchid had lied. Even though she, Didi, felt like a fool for believing her. Even though Didi had been betrayed.

But . . . she didn't *feel* betrayed.

Orchid grabbed a sunflower pillow and hugged it to her chest. She wouldn't make eye contact with Didi, and that was fine—Didi was never good with eye contact, anyway. It made her feel uncomfortable, vulnerable. Like the other person could see her every flaw.

"I won't tell anyone, if you don't want me to," Didi said. "I'm sure Greyson won't, either. He doesn't really talk to anyone at school, anyway. Unless he's forced to." She laughed lightly. When Orchid didn't respond, Didi cleared her throat and said, "Your dad seems nice."

Orchid smiled. She had a faraway look in her eyes, like Greyson had taken her spirit with him. Or maybe it was because she was here, in this temporary house in a temporary work camp, instead of filling the space around her with fanciful stories about first kisses and subway rides.

"He is," Orchid said. "He lets me pick a new name in every town. He arranges it beforehand, like 'Hey, my daughter goes by this nickname, so please call her Daisy or Lily or Orchid or whatever.' I think he does it because he feels guilty that we move all the time and my mom isn't here. But he doesn't know about all the other stuff. Like Victor and . . . everything."

Didi stared at the corkboard. All those welcome signs. "So Orchid isn't your real name?" she asked.

Orchid inhaled deeply and shook her head, still pressed against the pillow.

"It's always a flower, though," she said. "I was Lily in Baytown. And Daisy in Eagleton."

"Were the stories the same? About Victor and everything?"

"Sometimes. Sometimes different. And sometimes, I was just my real self. But . . . "

"But what?"

Orchid's eyes pooled with tears again.

Don't cry, Didi thought. *Please don't cry.*

Didi never knew what to do when people cried. She cried often, but always alone, where no one could see her. Tucked deep in her bed or in the shower. No witnesses. It was safer that way. Lonelier, yes, but safer.

"But I don't want to be me most of the time," Orchid said. Her sunflower pillow was wet. Didi saw it out of the corner of her eye.

"Why not?" Didi said. Her chest ached. Crying was contagious—if you cried with the right people, anyway. That's another reason she didn't like doing it.

Orchid shrugged. "Sometimes I just wish I was a different person. Or somewhere else. Faraway." She paused. "Sometimes I wish I could live a different life." She wiped her face with the back of her hand. "Does that ever happen to you?"

Orchid was looking at her. Didi could feel it. She always felt it when someone was looking at her.

She turned to her friend. Eye to eye.

"All the time," Didi said.

❀ *39* ❀

Janie had learned a long time ago that it was better to be Renni's friend than her enemy. She'd learned that back in second grade, on the day Renni pushed Baylee into the jungle gym.

Baylee's nose bled—Janie could still see the red blood against her white skin—and Mrs. Adams demanded to know what happened. Janie was the only witness, and she'd seen the whole thing. Baylee had said something (who knew what?), and Renni got angry and pushed her— no, *shoved* her—right into the steel bars. Janie could have said all this, but then she saw the way Renni's eyes pierced into hers. *If you tell,* those eyes said, *the next bloody nose will be yours.*

The best way to avoid getting shoved by Renni was to walk beside her. So that's exactly what Janie did.

Besides, Renni had a way of explaining things. "It was an accident," she'd say. "I didn't mean to." Or "I only did it because they did something to me first." Or "They deserved it" because of this reason or that reason.

And it's not like Renni was mean all the time. She could be fun, too. Janie, Renni, and Abby would stay up all night watching ridiculous videos on YouTube and they would laugh until they almost peed their pants. Renni picked the best scary movies. The three of them would huddle together in the dark, sharing an oversized bowl of popcorn. And Renni could be nice. She once gave Janie a set of tank tops that she didn't want anymore because she knew Janie liked them. And for Christmas two years ago, she gave Janie and Abby BFF necklaces. The three of them swapped secrets, most of which were still locked down to this day.

That was the thing about Renni lately, though. All those nice parts, all those fun parts, were fading away into hard lines and angles. Renni had never been *all* mean. *Mostly* mean, yes. But lately, "mostly" was becoming "always." Janie often felt like being Renni's friend was more of a job than anything. And, just like her job at the restaurant, she wasn't getting paid for it.

Janie thought about this as she scrubbed the burners to prep for the Saturday lunch crowd. She had her earbuds in, blasting music, even though her parents and Aunt Kiki told her not to wear them when she was working. When her music was interrupted by a FaceTime call, she tossed the scrub sponge aside, wiped down her hands, and pulled out her phone.

It was Renni.

She had a way of appearing as if she'd been conjured from Janie's thoughts. She was lying in the hammock of her backyard, squinting into the screen.

"Hey," Renni said. "I came up with a plan for the dance."

When Renni said she had a "plan" for something, it was never a good thing.

"Does that Orchid girl still think you're friends?" Renni asked.

Janie imagined Orchid, sitting by the creek, looking at her during Mirror Mirror and saying, "You have so much confidence, like you don't care what people think. I would love to be more like that."

But Janie *did* care. She would never admit it—she didn't even like to think about it, even to herself—but she *did* care. If she didn't, then why would Max's idiotic comment bother her so much? And why would she keep being friends with Renni, even though Renni somehow always made her feel worse about herself? And why did she care that everyone thought Orchid was the best thing that had ever happened to Fawn Creek?

Janie leaned against the restaurant's oversized stove and pushed those thoughts away. She fixed her face. That was something her mom always told her. She'd say, "Janie, fix your face!" And that meant to stop looking so sour or unhappy or pouty.

"Yeah, I guess," Janie said. "Why?"

Renni smiled and raised one eyebrow. At that moment she truly looked like a villain. It was almost funny.

Almost.

"Like I said," Renni continued. "*I have a plan.*"

A wave of anxiety moved through Janie's chest.

"What kind of plan?" she asked.

❀ *40* ❀

When Greyson walked into Mr. Agosto's classroom on Monday morning, there were four unanswered text messages from Dorothy on his phone. Asking if he was mad at her, asking him to call her, saying he didn't understand, wondering if he would talk to them at school. He'd never ignored a message from Dorothy in his life, but every time his screen lit up with a new message over the weekend, he'd nudged the phone away and focused on his sketches. He was going to design his own outfit by himself and so what if Dorothy didn't want to help? So what if he was on his own?

He avoided her eyes—everyone's eyes, really—when he sauntered into class. He made sure to enter the room one second before the bell so he wouldn't be forced to talk to her or Orchid. When he sat down, Dorothy whispered, "Hey," and he felt her eyes on the back of his head, but he didn't turn around.

What was he so mad about? Truth be told, he wasn't even sure. Yes, Orchid had lied. What was the big deal? She was a liar, so what. Everyone lied sometimes. Probably, if he'd really thought about it, if he hadn't been so swept up in her stories, he would have figured out she was lying earlier. And she seemed genuinely upset about it—or at least that she'd been caught, what with the crying and all. But you can't help how you feel, and the whole time he walked home through the field that afternoon, and the morning afterward, and the days that followed, he couldn't shake the trembling knot of anger that had settled deep into his chest.

Even now, he couldn't stop himself from shaking. His knee bounced up and down, up and down, under his desk. He crossed his arms. He thought he sensed Orchid's eyes shift in his direction, but he kept his face forward, glaring at Mr. Agosto's whiteboard as if it had put him under a spell.

"I'm sure all of you spent the weekend writing lyrical poetry in preparation for this week," Mr. Agosto said.

Shifts and groans and laughs. Monday morning

poetry was no one's idea of fun. Well. Except Mr. Agosto, apparently. He wrote two words on the board in big, capital letters: *I AM*.

"This week, we're going to work on our I Am poems," Mr. Agosto explained. "I know what you're thinking: 'What's an I Am poem, Mr. Agosto?'"

That wasn't what Greyson was thinking, of course. He was thinking: *Now who will I go to the dance with? Now who will I sit with at lunch?*

"Funny you should ask," Mr. Agosto continued, oblivious to the thirteen blank stares that blinked back at him. It was only Monday, but they were already desperate for the weekend, especially since it was the weekend of the dance.

Stupid dance, Greyson thought. *Stupid classroom. Stupid Agosto. Stupid town. Stupid life. Stupid poems. Stupid everything.*

His best friend since forever had been enchanted by stories full of lies—just as he had—and she had chosen those stories over him.

"I Am poems help us explore who we are," Mr. Agosto said. Greyson was half listening. Not even half listening. Fifteen percent listening. "The form follows a simple structure." He went back to the board. "Like this . . . "

Greyson still felt Dorothy's eyes on him. Her sad, quiet eyes.

Fine. Whatever. She liked the stories better than she liked him. Yes, *that's* why he was punishing her. *That's what this is about,* he thought, as his knee bounced up and down, up and down. He was mad at her for being so gullible. He was mad at her for *not* being mad. And he was mad at Orchid for not telling the truth. Why couldn't she just be herself? Who cared, anyway? Who cared about her sorry sack of stories?

He swallowed and focused on the board.

Mr. Agosto was writing something, but Greyson only saw letters, not words. He wasn't paying attention. He replayed Saturday morning in his head. All those photos of old signs and no friends and a mysterious mother.

He shifted in his chair.

He knew, deep down, in that place where he hid a million unspoken thoughts, ones that he wouldn't even admit to himself, he *knew* the real reason why he was angry. But maybe *angry* wasn't even the right word.

Hurt?

Disappointed?

Disenchanted?

Whatever the word was—and "every word matters," according to Mr. Agosto—there was an unspoken thought in the corner of Greyson's mind.

I wanted it to be true.

The kiss with Victor on the lock bridge.

The subway ride in New York City.

The hot springs of Iceland.

The monkeys on Phi Phi Island.

Greyson wanted it *all* to be true.

The other option wasn't an option.

Because if it wasn't true, the reality was this: Orchid was an ordinary kid, living in a small town, who had never been anywhere, had never seen anything, had never eaten a hot dog from a street vendor or stared up at the Eiffel Tower, and she'd probably go on like that, never going anywhere, never seeing anything, never escaping, just going on like that forever.

Just like him.

❀ *41* ❀

Orchid didn't lead Didi outside at lunch. Instead, Didi led them both to an out-of-the-way table in the corner. The cafeteria was too small to have real hidden nooks, but this corner table was usually unoccupied because it was furthest away from the doors and closest to the trash cans.

Orchid's tray carried two additional apples, as usual, one of which she tucked carefully in her backpack. Didi wondered where the monkey pin on her bag had really come from. A small shop in Texas? A gas station mini-mart? A store in Arkansas? Etsy? Amazon?

"Have you talked to Greyson today?" Orchid asked. She said it quietly, like she was afraid the question would burst into flames. Her hair fell soft and loose down her back.

Didi glanced toward their usual table, but Greyson wasn't there. She knew he wouldn't be. "I tried. He's ignoring me."

"I feel really stupid," Orchid continued. She sighed and stared at her taco boat. "And embarrassed."

Didi did, too, though she wasn't sure why. Sometimes it felt like embarrassment was contagious and she was uniquely susceptible to catching it.

"I understand," Didi said. "But there's no reason to feel that way. Not with me, anyway."

"He was right, you know," said Orchid. "I'm the one who's boring. Not Fawn Creek."

Didi pinched her straw just to have something to do. "I don't know about that," she said. "Yawn Creek is *pretty* boring."

Orchid smiled faintly and picked up her fork. Didi did, too. She wondered where Greyson was. Hiding in the bathroom? Sitting with a teacher, pretending he needed help with something? Didi thought of the texts she'd sent over the weekend. It wasn't right, really, for him to ignore her. She hadn't done anything wrong, had she? She was so lost in this question that her mind barely registered when Janie and Abby walked over and sat down—uninvited—with their trays.

Janie said, "We can't deal with Barn and Slowly today—"

Not Slowly, Didi thought. *Lehigh.*

"—so we figured we'd see what y'all were up to, and why you're sitting at the reject table."

Orchid shrugged. "Just a change of scenery."

"Where's Greyson?" Abby asked.

"Around," Didi replied.

Janie scooped a spoonful of fruit cocktail and said, "So. Are y'all still going to the dance? Doing the friend date thing?" She slipped the spoon into her mouth.

What did Janie care?

"Probably," Didi said.

"It's gonna be so much fun!" Abby said. Her smile was bright enough to light the entire room. "Janie and I are going shopping after school to get new outfits."

Please don't invite me. Please don't invite Orchid. Please go away.

Janie wiped her mouth with a napkin and laid it gently on her plate, not making eye contact. "What are you going to wear, Orchid?"

"I don't know," Orchid said. "I haven't even thought about it yet."

"You should wear your hair *exactly* like it is now," Janie said.

Abby furrowed her eyebrows. "That's random. Why

shouldn't she wear it up, like in those super-cute braid things she wore that one time?"

Janie shrugged. "I just think it looks really good when it's down, like it is now. That's all."

"Thank you," Orchid said. Her voice was quiet and uncertain. Didi figured she was thinking the same thing. *Go away, Crawford cousins. Shoo-shoo.*

"How are you going to wear your hair, Dorothy?" Abby asked.

Janie rolled her eyes. "What a stupid question. Dorothy wears her hair the same way every day. It hasn't changed since kindergarten."

"*Excuse me,*" Abby said. "I was trying to be nice."

Orchid reached over and squeezed Didi's hand.

"Didi may wear her hair differently," Orchid said. "Who knows?"

"Sure," Janie said, with biting sarcasm.

Dorothy imagined the other three girls with their beautiful, elaborate hair, and her, same old Didi—no, same old *Dorothy*—standing beside them, gazing through a veil of stringy brown strands and split ends.

Who knows? Maybe she'd surprise them.

Maybe she'd surprise them all.

❀ *42* ❀

Zucchini was a good dog. She never barked at people when they walked up to the house. She just ran toward the fence, tail wagging, like a big, slobbery welcoming committee. If you were in the backyard with Zucchini, you always knew when someone was coming up the walkway because she'd take off, ready to say hello.

That's how Greyson knew Dorothy and Orchid were there. He couldn't see them. He couldn't hear them. But the moment Zucchini picked up her head from Greyson's lap and bounded away, he knew. And there was no escape.

Why should he want to escape, anyway? He was the one who was mad at *them*, right?

For some reason, though, he suddenly had a desperate

desire to dig a hole and crawl into it. Instead, he stayed right where he was until he heard the sliding glass doors open and sure enough, there they were.

"Your mom let us in," Dorothy said.

She and Orchid joined him on the patio, even though he hadn't invited them. They sat in a row, on the cement, with their backs against the brick of the house, just like Dorothy and Greyson had done a million times before, only now no one was saying anything. Zucchini didn't seem to care about the tension—she just wanted someone to pet her. At the moment, that person was Orchid.

"I'm sorry, Greyson," Orchid said, after several seconds of silence. "Nothing I said came out right. I know Fawn Creek is its own town, and I know everyone is their own person. I just . . . " She paused. Scratched Zucchini absently behind the ears. "I guess I just didn't feel like *I* was my own person. Or, more like . . . I don't know." Zucchini inched closer to her and nuzzled under her chin. Orchid sighed.

That was all it took, really.

The frustration, anger, disappointment that Greyson had carried through the weekend fell away, draining off his shoulders like a waterfall.

"It's okay," Greyson said. "I understand."

He felt like crying—he really did—but he pushed the feeling away. *Quit acting like a little girl,* his father would say. No, he wouldn't cry, not even here, with people who were safe. Not out in the open where Trevor could appear at any moment. "I don't always like myself, either."

Orchid turned to him. "Why?" she said. "You're amazing."

Dorothy leaned forward. "I concur."

Greyson smiled. He rarely blushed—certainly not like Dorothy did—but he was blushing now. He could feel it.

"I think you're both amazing, too," he said. And before it got *too* awkward, before it got *too* mushy, he added: "But not as amazing as my outfit is going to be at the dance."

"You're really going to do it?" Dorothy asked, eyes shining.

"Do what?" asked Orchid.

"Greyson is designing his own clothes to wear to the dance," Dorothy said. "It's all sketched in his semi-secret notebook." She turned to him. "Did you decide to go with the purple?"

"Mulberry," Greyson corrected. "And yes. I just have to figure out . . . well, everything about how to make clothes. Including how to sew." He raised his eyebrows at Orchid. "Do you know how?"

"Me? No way," she said. "Why don't you ask your mom? Doesn't she have an entire sewing room?"

"Yeah, but . . . "

"But what?"

Greyson imagined how that would go. He'd ask his mother if she could teach him and she'd pause and get a look on her face, a look that said *Your father wouldn't like it* or *Wouldn't you rather go duck hunting?* Or *It's not really a guy thing, and you should be doing guy things,* and he would see all the gears turning as she tried to figure out the nicest way to tell her son that he needed to be more appropriate. Because even though his mother was never cruel like Trevor or biting like his father, she also wasn't reassuring.

"It's worth asking, right?" Orchid said.

They were all looking at him. Even Zucchini.

"Right, Greyson?" Dorothy said.

Greyson wasn't sure.

43

Greyson didn't grab his notebook on the way to the kitchen to talk to his mother, but Dorothy did. She snatched it up without a second thought and tucked it under her arm as the three of them made their way to Mrs. Broussard, who was unloading the dishwasher. She was placing a clean glass in the cabinet as they marched in.

"Hey," Mrs. Broussard said, scanning their faces. "What's up?"

Dorothy waited for Greyson to speak. When he didn't, she said: "We were wondering if you could help us—uh, help Greyson, that is—with something."

Mrs. Broussard leaned against the counter. "Of course." She hesitated. "Is something wrong?"

"No, not exactly," Dorothy replied.

Orchid stepped forward. "Can you teach Greyson how to sew?"

Mrs. Broussard raised her eyebrows and looked at the three of them, finally settling on Greyson. "You need to learn how to sew? Is this for a school project or something?"

"Yes," said Greyson.

"No," said Dorothy.

"Kind of," said Orchid.

"Let me rephrase the question," Mrs. Broussard said. "*Why* do you need to learn how to sew?"

Greyson looked at his feet. "Well. I don't *need* to, exactly . . . "

"Yes, he does," said Orchid. She elbowed Dorothy and motioned toward the notebook. Dorothy slipped it from under her arm and flipped through the pages. She hadn't realized how many sketches there were. When had he drawn all these?

"Wow," Dorothy muttered, mostly to herself. "These are amazing, Greyson."

"Thanks," Greyson said quickly, reaching for it. "But I didn't tell you to bring that. It's my private sketchbook."

Dorothy scarcely heard him. She was caught up in the sketches. Orchid, too. She peered at the penciled images and whispered, "How did you learn how to draw all these?"

"Which one is for the dance?" Dorothy asked, turning the pages. Her question was answered when she arrived at the page with "mulberry" written in the margins.

"Here it is," Dorothy said. She handed the notebook to Greyson's mother, who accepted it gingerly, like a hot plate that might burn her.

"What's this?" Mrs. Broussard said.

"Greyson designed it for the dance this weekend," Orchid said. She looped her arm around his waist.

Mrs. Broussard's eyebrows pinched together as she studied the drawing. "Oh . . . " she began.

Dorothy's heart pounded. She tried to catch Greyson's eye, but he was focused on his mother's expression.

"This is nice, but . . . there's no way you could get this all done by Friday," Mrs. Broussard finally said.

"Get what done by Friday?"

Trevor. He barged into the kitchen and grabbed a Sunkist from the fridge. When no one answered right away, he said, "Whatever. I'm gonna help Mrs. Moses pull some weeds," then headed out the door.

Orchid leaned her head on Greyson's shoulder and eyed the sketchbook. Mrs. Broussard was flipping through it.

"You must be so proud of him," Orchid said.

Mrs. Broussard looked up. "Yes. Trevor has always

been helpful in that way. Helping Mrs. Moses with her groceries, pulling weeds—"

Orchid lifted her head. "I meant Greyson."

"Oh," Mrs. Broussard said. "Yes." She cleared her throat. "I'm proud of both of my sons."

The room filled with silence.

"Can I have my notebook back?" Greyson said, after what felt like a decade.

Once it was in his hands again, he retreated from the kitchen without another word.

Dorothy and Orchid followed.

❀ *44* ❀

Dorothy apologized as soon as they were in his room. She launched into an avalanche of "I'm sorry" and "I wasn't thinking," but Greyson found himself oddly unfazed.

"It's okay," Greyson said. "They weren't really private."

The truth is, a piece of him *wanted* his mom to see his sketches—wanted *someone* to see them, at least—because he was proud of what he'd created. He had reason to be proud, didn't he? He designed all those clothes himself. He didn't know much about fabrics and sewing, not yet, and maybe he didn't even know anything about fashion, but he'd created *something*.

The three of them sat on the floor of his room, which hardly resembled the space of a twelve-year-old boy. The walls were bare. The furniture, bland and functional. Trevor had posters of country bands and hot girls on his walls. It's not like Greyson could tack a poster of Kate Middleton in her red Alexander McQueen double-breasted overcoat above his dresser. That's why he preferred the sewing room. He was more at home there, usually. But he didn't want to be there now.

"It was probably a stupid idea," Greyson said. He picked at the corner of his notebook.

"It's not a stupid idea at all. It's a brilliant, brave, and amazing idea," said Orchid.

Trevor has always been helpful. That's what his mother had said. Was it helpful when Trevor called him "Gayson"? Was it helpful when he pinched his arm so hard it left a bruise? Was it helpful when he introduced Greyson as his "sister"? Trevor could pull all the weeds in the universe and it wouldn't make him a nice person. Besides, Mrs. Moses always paid him for his time. It's not like he was *volunteering.*

Trevor has always been helpful.

What a joke.

"We can still do it," Dorothy said. "We might not be able to make *that* outfit, but we can come up with *an* outfit."

Greyson glanced toward his closet. He knew what was in it. He could provide an entire catalog if he wanted to. His closet was just as underwhelming as his room.

"My clothes are boring," Greyson said.

Orchid stood up and walked to the closet.

"The clothes might be boring right now, but that doesn't mean they have to stay that way." She put her hand on the closet door like it was a gateway to another world.

Two hours later, they stood in a sea of hoodies, T-shirts, and jeans, like human islands surrounded by an ocean of fabric and possibility. Four items were draped across Greyson's bed, along with his notebook, which was opened to a new sketch. They stared down at it, contemplative.

"I think it'll be amazing," Orchid said. "No. I don't *think*. I know."

Greyson imagined walking through the doors of the Grand Saintlodge Community Center. His heart banged in his chest.

The rumbling of Mr. Broussard's truck swelled in the distance.

Greyson shut his notebook. "Do you want to stay for dinner?" he asked. He immediately got to work picking up the clothes. His parents didn't care if he kept his room clean, but they'd definitely ask what he was up to if they saw every piece of clothing he owned all over the place, and he didn't want to navigate that question. "I have no idea what my mom's making."

"Nah, I better get home," Orchid said. "I'm already late."

"Do you want us to help you pick up?" Dorothy asked. She plucked an old T-shirt from the floor.

"I'll do it," Greyson said. He nodded toward the pile in his arms. "Just toss that on top."

His bedroom door opened as Dorothy tossed it in his direction.

Mrs. Broussard stood in the doorway. "What's going on in here?" she asked, scanning the mess.

Greyson threw the first armload of clothes into his open closet. He'd hang them up later. He just wanted to get everything back to normal. Nothing to see here.

"Finding something to wear for the dance," he mumbled.

"Do you want to stay for dinner?" Mrs. Broussard asked as Orchid and Dorothy made their way to the door. "We're getting takeout."

"No, thank you," they said, in unison.

"I'm already late," Orchid said.

"Do you want me to drive you home?"

"No, Didi and I are going to walk."

Mrs. Broussard raised her eyebrows. "Who is Didi?"

Orchid linked arms with Dorothy.

"I'm Didi," Dorothy said.

Greyson scooped up more clothes. He wished he could become someone else. Orchid and Dorothy came up with new names for themselves. Maybe he could, too. Who says he had to be Greyson? His parents chose that name for him. It's not like he had a say. Shouldn't people get to choose what they're going to be called for the rest of their lives?

He tried to conjure a new name for himself, but nothing came to mind. Just Greyson, Greyson, Greyson.

He turned back to his closet when his arms were full. Dorothy and Orchid left, and maybe he told them good-bye; he couldn't really remember, because he was trying to decide what name he'd choose for himself.

Alexander McQueen had a cool name. Maybe he could be Alexander Broussard. Maybe he'd create a whole new identity for himself if he ever made it to New York and became a real fashion designer.

Thinking of New York made him think of Orchid, that first day, when he asked if she was from Paris and she took a bite of her apple and said, "No, I'm from New York." He imagined himself saying that, years from now, when he was in his twenties. He would be at a fancy party somewhere faraway and someone would ask, "Where do you live?" and he'd say, "New York," real casual. Just like Orchid. But it would be true.

When he turned around, his mother was still there. He froze, like his feet were cement blocks. Was she going to have a talk with him? Tell him that boys didn't need to know how to sew?

She closed the door. Walked to the bed. Picked up his notebook.

He wanted to rip it away from her and hide in a deep, dark cave.

"You can't make this in a week, Sunbeam," she said, staring down at his mulberry sketch.

"I know," he said. "I don't want to make it anymore, anyway."

We came up with a different plan.

I didn't need you in the first place.

I have friends to help me.

"I'm not an expert seamstress," she said. "But I can teach you what I know." She spread her hands across the cover of his notebook and pressed her lips together, like she had more to say but wasn't sure how to say it.

Greyson didn't speak.

"I can teach you how to hem. Maybe you can earn some allowance as my assistant. Then you can buy your own fabric at Ann's in Saintlodge. I can take you next time I go," she said. "They have the best selections."

Ann's Fabrics. Rows and rows of endless patterns and textures, waiting to become something.

He swallowed.

"Okay," he said.

❀ 45 ❀

Janie watched Orchid all week. Orchid was a specimen to be studied, and Janie was the scientist. Actually, not a scientist. A predator, ready to pounce. She waited for the day when Orchid would lead them all outside at lunch. Regale them with stories of beach monkeys and Vietnamese noodles and Eiffel towers. That would be the fuel for the fire.

But Orchid wasn't leading anyone outside anymore.

Orchid hadn't told a single new story.

She wasn't even wearing her ridiculous flower.

She just wandered around with Dorothy and Greyson and acted *normal*. Like she wasn't the biggest fraud on the planet. Like she wasn't a pathetic little liar. Like she wasn't conning all of them, and for what? So she could feel important? Act like she was better than them? Janie wasn't going to let her get away with it.

"You can't let her go around acting like a princess," Renni had said on the phone last night. "She's making all of you look so *stupid,* and you're just letting it happen. Typical Yawn Creek. If I was there, I would've gone off on her *days* ago."

Renni had all the goods on Orchid. All the real information. Of course she did. She'd made it her business. Orchid wasn't from New York. She wasn't from anywhere that mattered. She'd never lived in Paris. She was a small-town girl with no money and no mother, who lived with her father in a temporary work camp.

Renni hadn't told anyone—just Janie. Because Renni trusted her. "I'm telling you because you're my best friend," Renni had said. "I'm keeping my mouth shut until the dance."

Renni had a plan for Friday night. She and Janie were the only ones who knew about it, besides Ethan and Hunter, the two guys from the football game.

"Now that I'm gone, you're the most popular girl in Fawn Creek," Renni had said, more than once. "And *this girl* thinks she can just prance her way in, pretend to be someone she's not, and everyone's just gonna *bow down?* No, thank you."

Renni had learned the truth from her father.

"When I asked if they were from New York, he *actually laughed*. He said they were as country as anyone," Renni said. "I can't believe she fooled all of you. I mean, does she even have a New York accent? Idiots."

No, Janie thought, *Orchid* didn't *have a New York accent,* now that she thought about it. Then again, she wasn't totally sure what a New York accent sounded like. And Orchid didn't have a Southern accent, either. She didn't seem to have an accent at all.

"People should be proud of where they're from," Renni continued. "Instead of making up *lies.*"

Janie thought that was ironic, since Renni tried to distance herself from Fawn Creek as much as she could. Renni even called Saintlodge her "hometown" now. *Technically, it's my hometown, because I was born in the hospital here,* she'd say to anyone who would listen. But that was only because there was no hospital in Fawn Creek. Whatever. Who cared? Renni was right about everything else, wasn't she? Orchid *had* lied. Not just about where she was from or where she'd been. Even her name was made-up. Her real name was so *common.* Plain. *Boring,* if you want to know the truth.

Janie thought of that name now, happy Renni had trusted her with the secret, as Mr. Agosto collected their

I Am poems. Janie passed hers forward—thankful to be rid of the stupid assignment, which Mr. Agosto had talked about all week (don't teachers have *lives*?)—and imagined how she would confront Orchid today, if given the chance.

Renni's plan would be put into place tonight, but Janie still wanted to prove that she could confront Orchid on her own.

Maybe today would be the day Orchid led them all outside again for another tall tale. And then Janie would burst her bubble. Perhaps she would go for the quiet attack, let Orchid make a bigger and bigger fool of herself.

Tell us more about your trip to Bangladesh, Orchid. I want to hear every detail. By the way, I heard the funniest thing the other day. I heard you moved here from Baytown, Texas. And before that you were in Oklahoma. And before that you were in Mississippi. And I think you've been to Alabama, right? Maybe you confused Elmdale, Alabama, for Paris, France? They're so similar!

Perhaps she would go for direct confrontation. Point her finger and shout, "You're a liar! Tell them the truth!" Maybe she could be a hero to them all. *Gather around, Baylee, Daelyn, Hallie. You, too, Barn and Slowly. Colt and Daniel, come closer. Max—you're a dumb-faced loser, but you can hear this, too. I have something important to share. Your hero, Orchid, is a liar and a con artist. And I'm pretty sure*

Greyson and Dorothy are in on it, too. They've all been making things up just to make you look stupid. Just to make you feel like white trash from a small town. What do you think about that, huh? Well? What do you think of "Orchid" now?

THE DANCE

❀ *46* ❀

Sometimes there's nothing more frightening than walking through a door.

Greyson imagined himself as the star of a movie. Or someone even more impressive. A person who had to Make an Entrance. Princesses, presidents, boxers, kings— they all made entrances. And this would be his.

Dorothy and Orchid stood on either side of him, elbows linked. He was suddenly convinced he'd made a grave error. But it was too late. Here they were, approaching the door, and now they were standing in front of it. More to the side, actually, because Greyson had hesitated and other kids were flowing past them. Kids they didn't recognize. Saintlodge kids, presumably. A few of them glanced his way, but most of them didn't seem to notice him. The air was hot and humid. Typical Louisiana.

"I should have worn my hair up," Orchid said. "It's hot."

Her hair was down, loose and flowy. She'd tucked a lily behind her ear. She was wearing a white dress, just like the one he imagined Emily Dickinson wore.

"It'll be cooler inside," Didi said, nudging Greyson. "You ready?"

"I think this might have been a really stupid idea," said Greyson.

"You look great," Orchid said. "Let's just go in."

Music thumped from inside the community center. They were fifteen minutes late, thanks to Mrs. Doucet's slow driving, so it was crowded already. There was a line at the check-in desk just down the corridor. Beyond that, the gym—now a dance floor—was mostly dark, with some flashing lights. Maybe no one would see him in the darkness.

Thank God they got a ride from Mrs. Doucet. Greyson couldn't imagine what Trevor would have said.

He couldn't imagine what the kids here would say, either.

Greyson took a deep breath.

"Okay," he said. "Let's go in."

Daniel + Hallie

"I think you have a drinking problem," Daniel said as he watched Hallie open her third Dr Pepper.

"I can't help it," she said. She took a long sip and hugged the can to her chest. "It's Dr Pepper, and it's free. Those are two of my favorite things."

Daniel smiled and motioned toward her shirt, which said "Ghosts Dance to Soul Music."

"Nice shirt," he said.

"Thanks." Sip. "Baylee and Daelyn said I shouldn't wear it because it's a Halloween shirt. I told them it wasn't a Halloween shirt; it's a *dance* shirt, and we're at a dance, so it only made sense."

Daniel nodded. "I appreciate your logic."

They weren't on a date, exactly. He'd asked her to the dance, sure, but they hadn't arrived together. They were dropped off separately and agreed to meet at the soda station, just outside the gym. They hadn't crossed the threshold yet, mostly due to Hallie's Dr Pepper addiction. Was she stalling? Daniel wondered. Maybe because once they were in the gym, they might have to dance or hold hands or something that showed the world that they were here together, rather than two random seventh graders out for free soda.

She didn't seem nervous, but who could say? He

wondered if he seemed nervous to her. He certainly *felt* nervous.

"Are Max and Colt coming?" Hallie asked.

The sign-in table wasn't far from them. The line had grown and now snaked down the corridor and out the front door. Saintlodge kids, mostly. Daniel recognized a few sixth graders from Fawn Creek, but just about everyone else was unfamiliar.

"Yeah," Daniel said. "Max is already inside. He didn't want to get dropped off with Colt because he was worried it'd look like they were a couple or something."

"Max is such an idiot." Sip. "No offense."

None taken, Daniel thought.

"Are you almost done with your drink? Because if you have another one, I might have to call a support group or something," he said.

She tilted the Dr Pepper absently back and forth, her eyes studying the line of people. Music from the gym reverberated under Daniel's skin. There was something hypnotic about music blaring through loudspeakers. Like it had the power to make you a different person or something.

"I have a confession," she said. She bit her lip. Glanced at him. Glanced away.

He swallowed. Uh-oh.

"Okay," he said. He laughed nervously. "Should I get a priest?"

She smiled. "It's just . . . I don't really, like, *know* how to dance. I mean, I once got hooked on the Hokey Pokey, but I turned myself around."

Daniel laughed. "That's a shame, because I *really* know how to cut a rug. When the music hits me, watch out. Clear the dance floor," he said. "Guess I'll have to find a different dance partner."

She laughed as he craned his neck toward the check-in line, pretending like he was searching for her replacement.

His eyes caught on a trio of familiar faces. "Hey, there's Greyson and them," he said.

Hallie followed his gaze.

Daniel wiped his hands on his jeans. Should he try to hold Hallie's hand at some point?

"What's Greyson wearing?" said Hallie.

Daniel had never been one to notice anything anyone was wearing, but he noticed now. It looked super haphazard. Like Greyson had all these different items of clothing and he patched them together into one big chaotic mess. Or like someone dressed him in the dark.

Then again, what did Daniel know about fashion? Nothing.

"Greyson's always been an original," Daniel said.

Hallie laughed. One single *ha!* At that moment, Daniel thought it was the best sound in the world.

"You're right," Hallie said. "He's an original."

Greyson, Dorothy, and Orchid paid their money, got their hands stamped, and walked around the table, heading in their direction. It was difficult—if not impossible—to saunter by fellow Fawn Creekers without saying hello, or at least nodding or waving, so Daniel figured they approached more out of obligation than anything.

Now that they were closer, Daniel saw the entirety of Greyson's outfit. There *was* something kinda cool about it. Maybe because it was unlike anything Daniel had ever seen.

"Hey," Orchid said.

Dorothy's skin was tinted red under the collar of her shirt.

"Hey," Hallie said. She tossed her soda in the nearby trash can. "I love your clothes, Greyson. They make a statement."

Greyson's face relaxed. He smiled. "Thanks, Hallie," he said. "I like yours, too."

"Question," Daniel said. "Would you categorize Hallie's shirt as a Halloween shirt or a dance shirt?"

Hallie stood up straight and opened her arms wide, putting her shirt up for scrutiny.

"Definitely a dance shirt," Greyson said.

Dorothy and Orchid agreed.

"See?" Hallie said. "Daelyn and Baylee don't know what they're talking about."

Dorothy glanced toward the gaping entrance of the gym. "Are they here?" she asked, her voice quiet. "I was wondering who else came."

Hallie nodded. "They're inside, secretly applying makeup."

"Max is in there, too," Daniel said. "I mean, not secretly applying makeup. Just, you know, in the gym. And Janie and Abby are here somewhere. I also saw some lowly sixth graders."

The music changed tempo. Upbeat. Daniel wasn't a guy who danced—like, ever—but there was something about it that made him want to go inside and test the waters. Maybe he and Hallie could make fools of themselves together.

Orchid eyed Dorothy and Greyson. "Let's go in!" she said. "We have to make this a night to remember."

She extended her hand to Dorothy. Dorothy took it, and extended hers to Greyson. He smiled and wrapped his hand around hers.

Well. If *they* could do it . . .

Daniel reached his hand out to Hallie with his eyebrows raised.

She took it.

❀ ❀ ❀

Janie + Abby

The music was loud, but once your ears adjusted, it was easy to have a conversation. Even better, the thumping of the bass camouflaged your secrets.

All but one set of bleachers had been put away to make room for the dance floor, and most of the seats were occupied by people who weren't interested in dancing or were gathering the courage to ask someone to dance or waiting for someone to ask *them*. Many were also just gossiping, which is what Janie had in mind when she pulled Abby to one of the corner sections. It was a relief that Barn and Slowly hadn't come; they would have been deadweight, lingering around Janie and Abby because they had no one else to talk to. Neither Barn nor Slowly would've had the courage to venture out and talk to any other girls.

Under different circumstances, Janie would be focused on one thing: boys. She dreamed about someone to asking her to dance. A *slow* dance. She wanted to perch her hands on some cute boy's shoulders while they swayed to some super-romantic song. If you'd asked her weeks ago what her goal was, that's what she would have said. But now she had a different goal. She hadn't told Abby anything about it yet because she knew Abby wouldn't approve, but Renni would get there soon, and Abby needed a head's up. She didn't need to know everything, but she needed to know *something*. It was only fair.

"What's this important thing you have to tell me? Is it about Max? I saw him come in and I think he looked at you," Abby asked, the moment they sat down. Abby had worn more makeup than usual and she looked so pretty that Janie was almost jealous. Almost.

"No. Who cares about Max?" Janie said, but even as the words traveled out of her mouth, she wondered if it was true. Had he been looking for her?

"Well?" Abby leaned forward. "What then?"

Janie looked around to make sure no one was eavesdropping. They were surrounded by kids from Saintlodge. Clusters of unfamiliar faces—laughing, taking selfies, posting stories—flashed under the multicolored strobe lights. The music thumped through the bleachers.

"It's about Orchid," said Janie.

"Ooh!" Abby said. "What about her?"

Janie scooted closer. "Renni did some digging and uncovered some interesting information about our friend from 'New York.'"

Abby frowned.

"For one thing," Janie continued. "She's not even *from* New York. And not only isn't she from there, she's never even gone." Janie counted on her fingers: "Same for Thailand, Vietnam, Paris, and whatever other places she's made up."

Abby blinked.

"She's basically just a liar," Janie said. "She's been lying to everyone. Trying to make us look stupid. Making us feel like poor white trash." These were Renni's words, not hers. But they were hers, too, in a way.

Abby glanced at her lap. "She never made me feel like poor white trash."

"Good," Janie said. "Because *she's* the one who's white trash. She's dirt-poor. Her dad makes, like, *nothing*. They live in a work camp. And her mother . . . " Janie paused for effect.

"What about her mother?"

Janie cupped her hand around her mouth and leaned toward Abby's ear. "Total drug addict junkie," she whispered. "In *prison*. For like, a *life sentence*, practically."

The last part—about the life sentence—was a little made-up, but so what? It could be true, for all Janie knew. Orchid's mother was definitely locked up. Renni's dad had said so. Maybe it was for a month, maybe it was for life. Who cared? The important thing was, everything Janie had said was mostly true.

Abby's eyes widened. "In prison? Really?"

Janie nodded gravely.

Abby stared at the bleachers below them, as if she was focusing on something and nothing at the same time. "Poor Orchid," she said.

Poor *Orchid*?

"Don't fall for her tricks," Janie said. "I almost did, and I would've been reeled in just like the rest of you. It doesn't matter what's going on in your life. You can't just go around *lying* to people. Just *making things up*. Right?"

"I guess."

"It's not okay to *lie,* is it?"

"Well. No. But—"

"But nothing." Janie narrowed her eyes. "Orchid isn't even her real name, you know."

"What's her real name?"

Janie opened her mouth to answer, but her phone buzzed instead. She pulled it out of her back pocket.

Renni had arrived.

Baylee + Daelyn

The bathrooms of the community center weren't exactly made for massive primping, so Baylee and Daelyn had to find their way to the mirrors with their secret stash of makeup by nudging other girls out of the way. They did it kindly—as kindly as anyone could nudge—and squeezed as close together as possible so they could share the one pathetic mirror over the sink. It wasn't an ideal way to apply makeup, but it was the best they could do. Neither of their parents allowed makeup of any kind.

They skipped the foundation. Too messy in such a small space. Instead they focused on eyeliner, mascara, and lipstick. Their unpracticed attempts, coupled with all the other activity bustling around them, meant it took more time than they had anticipated. Daelyn finished first, and she felt like she might jump out of her skin waiting on Baylee. Music thumped through the walls.

"Hurry *up*," Daelyn said. "I wanna dance."

Baylee steadied her hand to apply lipstick. "I didn't rush you when you were doing your makeup, Dae."

"That's because you didn't have to."

The door opened and a trio of girls spilled in, laughing, bringing a burst of perfume with them. One of the girls stepped into an empty stall while the other two checked their reflections.

"I swear, that kid's outfit is over-the-top. Like, could he be any more desperate for attention?" the girl in the stall said.

The other two—a brunette and a blonde—fiddled with their hair.

"Who dresses that way *on purpose*?" the brunette said. "Seriously. *How* does he think that looks good? I hope he doesn't ask anyone to dance because she'll laugh in his face."

"Something tells me he wouldn't ask a *girl* to dance," the blonde said.

"Ew! Gross."

Daelyn turned away from the girls and studied Baylee. Who took this long to apply lipstick?

"Anyway," the blonde continued. "He's obviously one of those kids from Fawn Creek." Satisfied with her appearance, she crossed her arms and leaned against the wall. "You can tell which ones are from Fawn Creek because they look like they belong in an institution."

"Ohmygod, Sofie, you're so mean!" her friend said, stifling a laugh. She glanced at Baylee and Daelyn.

Daelyn imagined stabbing this Sofie in the face with her eyeliner pencil. Instead, she said a prayer of forgiveness. A quick one.

Baylee finished her lipstick just as the third girl came out of the stall. When the girl made a beeline for the bathroom door, Baylee called out, "You forgot to wash your hands!" and laughed as Sofie and her friends disappeared into the darkness of the gym.

Max + Colt

Colt regretted coming.

Max had gotten him all riled up, talking about the Saintlodge girls they'd meet, but Colt was already bored, and the only person he'd talked to so far was Max. They leaned against the wall near the DJ, acting like it was their plan to lean against *this very wall*, but Colt could only think about all the other places he'd rather be. Saintlodge High had a football game at their stadium a few miles away; he'd much rather be there. Or he and Max could have gone to the movies or something. But being here, surrounded by Saintlodge kids he didn't know, and girls he was too scared to talk to, made him feel awkward and out of place. And Michael Colt wasn't used to feeling awkward and out of place.

To make matters worse, Renni had just texted him to say she was here. When he didn't reply, she wrote, *I'm here with another guy. I just wanted you to know so you wouldn't be surprised.*

He didn't care—not even the slightest bit. But it would have been nice if he had a girl with him, too. Just so Renni wouldn't know that she'd won.

Won what? He had no idea.

"The girls here are lame," said Max. He had to practically yell because they were so close to the speakers. "I thought Saintlodge girls would be better."

They watched groups of girls walk by.

"I don't see anyone here worth asking to dance," Max said.

"Mm-hm," said Colt.

Anyone with a brain could see that Max was afraid to talk to any girls—especially ones he didn't know. It was much easier for him to decide they weren't worth talking to than admit that he was too scared to talk to them.

Colt eyed the crowd. There were lots of pretty girls around. New faces. In Fawn Creek you spent most of your life looking at the same people day after day after day. But at this moment, there was a new face every second.

He wondered if that's what it was like for Orchid when she lived in New York.

Speaking of which—

There she was.

With Greyson and Dorothy, not surprisingly. They were walking toward the bleachers, looking for a place to sit. As the crowd moved and they came into clearer focus, Colt saw Greyson's outfit.

What was he wearing?

"There's that girl," Max said.

He usually called Orchid "that girl" or "the new girl," like he was way too cool to remember her name, even though everyone knew *everyone's* name. Especially Orchid's.

"What the—" Max said, and Colt knew he was looking at Greyson, too.

Colt's phone lit up, like a beacon in the dark.

Renni was FaceTiming him.

Great.

His thumb hovered over the ignore button and he was ready to push it, when he looked up and saw her approaching. Her eyes were on her phone. Then they were on him.

She hung up and kept coming his way.

Colt cursed under his breath, but Max managed to hear it.

"What's up?" he said.

"The Monster," Colt said.

His pet name for Renni, which he only used with Max and Daniel.

Ten seconds later the Monster was in front of them. She'd really gone all out for the dance. Hair piled high on top of her head. Colt never understood why girls wanted their hair to look messy on purpose, but what did he know?

She was also wearing makeup. Way more makeup than he'd ever seen on her. Her lips were painted pink. They sparkled like glitter. Even though the gym was fairly dark, Renni's mouth seemed like the brightest—and loudest—object in the room.

"Michael!" she said, practically screaming. She always called him Michael, ever since they'd started going together, even though no one called him Michael. He was Colt. Always Colt. "There you are!"

Colt mumbled something.

Renni stepped forward. She smelled like fruit. Too much fruit.

"Hey," Max said, even though she hadn't even looked at him. "Who're you here with?"

He was hoping she was with girlfriends from Saintlodge, no doubt.

"Janie, Abby, and my boyfriend Ethan," Renni said, her eyes cutting back to Colt when she said "boyfriend."

"Oh," said Max.

Colt wondered where this "boyfriend" was since he didn't seem to be anywhere around. And if she was with her boyfriend, why was she talking to him? "What do you want?" he said.

Renni swatted his arm. "Rude!" She looked around conspiratorially, even though no one was paying attention to them. "I need to ask you for a favor."

Baylee and Daelyn emerged from the hallway that led to the bathrooms. They waved at Colt. He waved back—a small, casual wave that he hoped Renni wouldn't notice. Renni didn't like the God Squad, and he was pretty sure the feeling was mutual.

"What kind of favor?" Colt said.

The smell of Renni's fruity perfume was suddenly nauseating.

"I need you to ask 'Orchid'"— she used air quotes—"to go outside with you."

"What? Why?" Colt wasn't sure what he had expected, but it wasn't this.

"Just do it for me. Ask her to go for a walk or something. And then meet up with us by the giant oak tree with the lights on it."

"Who's 'us'?"

Renni huffed. "Just do it."

Max leaned forward. "Why? What's going on?"

"It doesn't matter," Colt said. "I'm not doing it. Why would I randomly ask Orchid to go for a walk with me?"

"Because you *like* her," Renni replied. "At least, that's what I heard."

"I've talked to her, like, once in my entire life," Colt said. "I'm not gonna walk up and ask her to go outside with me like some sort of weirdo. Besides, who does that? Who asks someone to take a *walk* with them?"

Renni huffed again. "Come on. Just do it."

"Why don't *you* ask her?" Max said.

"She doesn't know me," Renni said. "*And* she doesn't like me."

"Find someone else," Colt said. "Not interested."

The music changed tempo. Kids scattered from the dance floor, leaving only a few couples behind. One of them was Daniel and Hallie. Hallie put her hands on Daniel's shoulders. They swayed back and forth, not making eye contact.

Colt had never danced with a girl before. Maybe he'd ask someone. Not Renni. But someone. If only Renni would go away, he could concentrate.

He scanned the crowd. His eyes snagged on Greyson again. How could they not? And then, Orchid. But he wasn't really into her anymore. When she showed up at Fawn Creek, she'd been shiny and new and mysterious, but now she was just another girl. Not quite familiar, but not mysterious, either. Dorothy was sitting with them, a slight smile on her face. At least it *looked* like a smile. It was hard to tell from this distance, with this lighting.

He didn't want to ask Orchid to dance. But he wanted to ask someone.

"Hello?" Renni said, waving her hand in front of his face. "I'm *talking*."

Sure enough, she'd been blabbing away this whole time while his mind wandered. And so what? He didn't want to be in this conversation anyway.

"I told you, I'm not doing it," Colt said.

Renni crossed her arms. "Are you *scared*? Is that it?"

"Grow up," Colt said. He couldn't see Daniel and Hallie anymore. A few other couples had braved their way to the dance floor.

"I have to get 'Orchid' outside, away from her two parasites for, like, five minutes," Renni said. Her voice reminded Colt of his youngest sister, who was four.

"Why do you keep doing those stupid air quotes?" Max asked.

Renni smiled. "You'll find out soon enough," she said. She blinked up at Colt. "I need to talk to her about something important and her two *girl*friends can't be there. It's private. I need someone to take her away from them."

"Not my problem," said Colt.

Orchid appeared to be having fun. Greyson and Dorothy did, too. They were laughing. If Greyson noticed all the looks people were giving him, he didn't seem to care.

Renni took a big, deep breath, as if she were preparing for a full-on tantrum.

"Please," she said. She raised her eyebrows and actually *batted* her eyelashes. At least that's what it seemed like. "If you go over there and ask Orchid to take a walk with you, I will leave you alone for the rest of the night. I *promise.* Just do this one thing for me. Just this *one thing.* Please?"

And then she repeated it over and over, like a mantra smothered in too-sweet fruit body spray.

"Please? Please? Please? Please?"

Didi + Orchid

"People are laughing at me," Greyson said.

He didn't sound defeated or disappointed. Just observant.

And he was right. Lots of kids walked by and didn't even notice him. But those who did? It was the same thing on repeat. A glance, a double take. Then whispers and giggles. Didi wanted to reassure him—*No, no, people aren't laughing at you*—but the truth was, they were, and they all knew it. It felt worse to pretend like it wasn't happening.

"So what?" Orchid said. "Let them laugh. We can laugh, too."

"There's plenty of material," Greyson said, his eyes on the dance floor, which was crowded with couples moving to the *thump-thump-thump* of the music.

"Not at *people*," Orchid said. She was sitting between them, eyes sparkling. "I have a much more original way to make us laugh. *If* you can handle it." She paused. "Can you handle it?"

Greyson nodded.

Didi nodded.

The music walloped into Didi's ears and all the way to her toes. It simultaneously made her want to dance and stay still. The entire scene was a sensory overload. All these people she didn't know. All this loud music. All these lights.

But as long as Greyson and Orchid were nearby, she would be okay.

"Okay, here goes," Orchid said. She took a deep breath, closed her eyes, and said, "Knock, knock."

Didi and Greyson exchanged looks.

"Who's there?" Greyson said.

"Needle."

"Needle who?"

"Needle little help getting to the dance floor?"

Orchid's smile grew into a loud, harmonious laugh.

Greyson and Didi groaned, but they couldn't help it— they laughed, too.

Orchid elbowed both of them. "One of you go next."

Didi racked her brain for a joke, any joke. But she wasn't much of a comedian. Besides, she was distracted now because Renni was walking past them. She scanned Greyson's outfit and laughed behind her hand as she breezed by.

She was alone, at least, which made her slightly less dangerous. But only slightly. Didi watched her until she disappeared into the crowd.

"Who's there?" Orchid was saying, eyes on Greyson.

Apparently neither of them had paid any attention to Renni.

"Gladys," Greyson replied.

Didi knew this one. He'd told it to her before.

"Gladys who?" Orchid said.

Greyson shrugged. "Gladys the weekend—we don't have to go to school!"

Orchid's laugh soared into the air above them.

She and Greyson traded back and forth a few more times—*"What did Delaware? Her New Jersey!" "What did the man say when he visited the mirror factory? I could totally see myself working here!" "Why do cows wear bells? Because their horns don't work"*—until Orchid finally pressed a knuckle softly into Didi's thigh and said, "Your turn, Didi. Tell us a joke!"

Didi waited for the warm rush of embarrassment.

She waited for the red dread to crawl up her throat.

But neither of those things happened.

Instead, she said, "Why are leopards not good at hide-and-seek?"

She never had the chance to deliver the punch line, though, because all eyes turned to Michael Colt, who had somehow silently appeared before them. His smile was nervous. Cautious. He had his hands in his pockets. He was tall. So tall. The three of them looked up. He looked down. Didi was suddenly aware that the music had changed tempo at some point. It was a slow song now.

Oh, God. Colt was going to ask Orchid to dance.

What would she say? She'd probably say yes. Why not?

"Hey," Colt said. He cleared his throat.

They all said "Hey," one after the other.

"I was wondering . . . " Colt said. "Um . . . "

Awkwardness swelled all around them.

"I already know what you're going to say," Greyson said, grinning. "You want to know where I got my clothes, right?" He laughed.

Colt laughed, too. Nervously. Good-naturedly.

"Well, yeah . . ." Colt said. "Obviously." His eyes darted from Greyson to Orchid. Didi looked at Orchid, too. She wanted to see her friend's face when he asked her.

"But, really . . ." Colt continued. "I just wanted to know if you, ah, if you . . . *maybe* . . . wanted to dance?"

Orchid's face lit up. Brighter than the sun, it seemed like. But she didn't answer right away. She turned to Didi instead, smiling from ear to ear.

"Well?" Orchid said.

Greyson was looking at Didi, too. He looked ready to leap out of his seat.

"Well what?" Didi said.

Did Orchid want her permission or something?

"Colt asked you a question," Orchid said.

Wait—what?

Didi broke her eyes away from Orchid.

Her entire body felt warm, like it was going to burst into flames.

What was going on?

Colt was looking at her. At *her*.

"Do you want to?" he asked. He jerked a thumb toward the dance floor and Didi couldn't be sure, but—yes, yes, she was sure, now that she looked closer, she was sure—there were slight patches of red on his neck. Light. Rosy. Difficult to see in the dark, but there.

The red dread.

On Michael Colt's neck.

Because he was nervous.

Asking her to dance.

"Uh," Didi said. "Yes."

And Colt reached out his hand, just like in the movies, to escort her onto the dance floor, but at that moment—wouldn't you know it?—the song ended and the music swept into something faster, and all those groups of friends who had to evacuate for the couples swarmed back out.

"Guess I waited too long," Colt said, putting his hand in his pocket. He smiled. It was a shaky smile.

"Come back for the next slow song," Orchid said. "We'll be here."

"Okay," Colt said. He waved—half waved—and the moment he turned, Greyson reached across Orchid to smack Didi's leg. He mouthed *ohmygod ohmygod ohmygod,* which was exactly what Didi had been thinking.

Didi was ready to dissect the entire incident, even though it had just happened, and wanted to ask if they really thought he'd come back, and she would have done all that—the three of them would have done all that—if Janie and Abby hadn't sauntered up to them with fake smiles plastered on their glittery faces.

"Hey," Janie said.

"Hey," said Abby.

They all said "Hey," one after the other.

Janie was giving them direct eye contact, but Abby seemed shifty. She glanced from her feet to Orchid to the exit. Something was going on, no matter how hard Janie tried to fake smile.

"What're y'all up to?" Janie asked.

Greyson opened his arms and gestured to himself. "This," he said. "Clearly."

"Interesting ensemble," Janie said. "*Very* original. I love that you're courageous enough to just *be yourself.* You know?" She turned to Didi. "You, too, Dorothy. I love that you didn't change one thing about yourself for the dance. Same hair, same clothes, same everything. You're just so comfortable being *you.*"

Greyson narrowed his eyes at her.

Janie lowered her voice. "Anyway," she said, turning her attention to Orchid. "I was wondering if I could talk to you outside for a sec. *In private.*"

Orchid frowned. "Why?"

"Well, I can't tell you right now," Janie said. "That's why I have to do it in private." She paused. "It's about a personal problem I'm having."

"Why do you need Orchid's help?" Greyson said. "Isn't that what Abby and Renni are for?"

Janie widened her smile. "I'll explain it once we're outside, *Orchid.* Promise. We'll be back in, like, five minutes."

Didi swallowed. Her heart thundered. *Don't go. Don't go. Don't go.* But Orchid stood up anyway and followed Janie and Abby outside.

"I'll be right back," she said, over her shoulder.

Didi and Greyson watched her leave.

🏵 *47* 🏵

Janie's heart banged in her chest. You couldn't tell from the outside, but she was *nervous*. More nervous than she'd ever been in her entire life. The funny thing was, she hadn't expected to feel this way. She hadn't expected her hands to shake. She hadn't expected her throat to turn dry. She hadn't expected Abby's glare to bother her as much as it did.

Abby didn't even know about the plan. Janie hadn't told her. But she knew something was up. And something *was* up. Renni had it all mapped out. And Janie had been on board. She'd agreed to it, even just a few minutes ago, when Renni told her that Colt "punked out" and Janie would have to get Orchid outside on her own.

And she'd done it, hadn't she? Here they were, walking to the giant oak tree. The one with the lights on it. Janie couldn't see anyone standing underneath, but it was dark, so who could tell? Besides, the trunk was wide enough to hide behind. Renni was there in the darkness, no doubt.

They'd walked out the door, down the sidewalk, then veered toward the oak tree before Orchid asked where they were going.

"Yeah," Abby said. Her voice sounded defiant. "Where *are* we going, Janie?"

Janie didn't want to say too much. She was worried her voice would sound shaky and suspicious. *Turn around. Forget the whole thing. Don't do it.* Each word, each syllable, reverberated from the top of her head to her toes, like a cold shower of regret. Regret for what, though? She hadn't done anything wrong. They weren't even at the tree. But then, just like that, they were.

"We need to talk to you about something," Janie said. The "we" meant her and Abby, but Abby wasn't acting like a partner at all. She was standing next to *Orchid.* Traitor. Janie crossed her arms to keep her insides still.

"About what?" Orchid said. Her eyebrows pinched together. She frowned. She glanced back at the community center. "Let's go back. It's too dark out here."

Orchid knew she was in trouble; Janie could tell by the look on her face.

Janie swallowed. She'd practiced what she was going to say. She'd rehearsed it over and over. Now it was go time. Say your lines. Say your lines. *Say your lines.*

"About what a liar you are," Janie said. She blurted it out. It sounded much more biting and confident than she expected.

Remember what a liar she is, Janie reminded herself.

Remember that Orchid isn't even her real name.

Remember that she deserves what's coming to her.

Orchid took a step back. She cupped her hands in front of her and kneaded her fingers.

"I don't—" she said.

She paused when Renni emerged from the other side of the trunk with Ethan beside her. He was wearing a backpack. He slipped it off his shoulder and dropped it at his feet.

Orchid looked from the backpack to Ethan to Renni to Janie to Abby and back again, like this was a puzzle she was desperate to solve. But she didn't have all the pieces yet.

Janie did, though.

Renni did.

Even Ethan.

"What's going on?" asked Orchid, trying to smile, trying to act casual, like she was among friends.

"Yeah," Abby said, her voice quiet and soft. "What's going on?"

Renni took one step toward Orchid. Then two.

Janie's heart walloped. She'd imagined this scenario—had planned it with Renni—but now that it was unfolding, it felt wrong, it felt scary, it felt like a mistake. But she couldn't find the words to say so. She couldn't even open her mouth. It was clamped shut. She'd forgotten how to speak.

"You're a liar," Renni said, eyes level with Orchid.

Renni didn't look afraid at all.

How was that possible?

"You lied to everyone," Renni said. "You thought you could come here and just make up stories and we'd all believe them because we're some ignorant small-town hicks?"

"No," Orchid said. Her chin trembled. Her hands twisted and twisted.

"You're just as country as the rest of us. You know that, don't you? You're just a piece of sorry white trash. You don't even have a *mother*. And somehow you thought you were better than us?" Renni glanced around. "None of *our* mothers are junkie prostitutes. Only yours."

Orchid was silent. Her eyes pooled.

"Stop, Renni," said Abby. But she said it so quietly that the words escaped into the night air, like they had never existed.

"You think you're so much better than us?" Renni asked.

Orchid shook her head.

When Renni reached for her, she flinched, but rather than strike her across the face, Renni plucked the flower from her hair. "You think you're some kinda fairy freaking princess?" Renni dropped the flower and stepped on it.

"No," Orchid said. It was a sad, sorry syllable. A quiet slide of tears escaped with it.

Janie desperately wanted to be back inside, with the lights and the people, but it all seemed so far away now, as if ten miles separated them from the dance.

This is a mistake, she thought. *This is a mistake*. But Renni said Orchid deserved it. *Orchid is a liar*, Renni had said. And that was true, right? Renni had said Orchid was prancing around, acting like she was better than them. Treating them like poor white trash.

But that wasn't what happened, was it?

Janie looked at Orchid's face. She saw her at the creek, saying, "It's called Mirror Mirror. Do you want to play?" She saw her at the football game. "Are you okay?"

But she *had* lied. She had lied to all of them. Didn't that mean something? Shouldn't she pay for that?

"I want to go back, please," Orchid said. Her voice sounded small and young, like Mee-Wee's, which made Janie think of Mee-Wee with the flower in her hair.

Janie was going to say it, just like Abby had—"Stop, Renni," she would say—and she'd say it loudly, loud enough for the whole world to hear. But when she opened her mouth, nothing came out.

Then the scissors appeared.

Ethan slipped them out of his bag and handed them to Renni.

"What's going on?" Abby said. Louder now. Alarmed.

When Orchid caught sight of the scissors, she turned to run, but Ethan was ready for her. He grabbed her from behind, arms wrapped tight, and pulled her right back to where she'd been standing before.

Abby ran, too, but there was no one to catch her.

Orchid's face was wet now, like she'd smeared the tears across it and made it shine. She couldn't move. Her arms were trapped at her sides. She tried to kick, but the attempts were feeble, and finally she stopped and looked directly at Janie. The message was clear. *Help me, Janie.*

But Janie's mouth was still clamped shut as Renni raised the scissors.

"We believe in justice," Renni said. "When you do wrong, you have to pay."

In a quick motion—so quick that no one expected it; so quick that Ethan, Janie, and Orchid flinched in unison—Renni grabbed a thick lock of Orchid's hair and yanked it toward her. She opened the scissors and shoved the hair between the blades. They weren't supposed to *really* cut it. That wasn't the plan. "We'll just scare her," Renni had said. "We won't actually do anything." But the look in Renni's eyes made Janie's heart race.

Orchid made a sound. Something like a howl, something like a cry, something like a plea.

"Wait!" Janie said, surprising herself.

Ethan cursed. "What do you mean, wait?" His arms were skinny, but strong. He was holding tight. There was a look on his face—Janie wasn't sure how to describe it—but he almost looked *pleased*. Like he was enjoying it. Renni looked that way, too, holding the scissors close to Orchid's face. So close.

Janie cleared her throat. She didn't know what she was going to do or say. She just knew that she needed to get the scissors away from Renni and Ethan. She inhaled and said, "I'll do it." When Renni didn't move, Janie added, "*I'm* the one who's had to listen to all her stories."

Renni waited a moment before she released Orchid's

hair. Then she gave Janie the scissors.

"Cut it close to the scalp," Renni said. She turned toward Orchid. "Don't worry, your hair is *insured*, right? We'll see how valuable it is once we cut it all off."

"But—" Janie said, though she couldn't complete the sentence.

Keep the scissors away from everyone, she told herself. *Tell Ethan to let Orchid go. Forget the whole thing.*

"Don't chicken out," Renni snapped. "Cut it. *Really* cut it."

Janie reached her hand into Orchid's hair, waiting for the moment that her courage would build to a crescendo. But even as she told herself to *tell Ethan to let Orchid go* and *end this whole thing,* she placed a lock of Orchid's hair against the palm of her hand. She stared at it. The scissors were so heavy and so light. Orchid's eyes sparkled. Other than that little howl, she hadn't made a sound.

Renni said something—Janie wasn't sure what—then Ethan swore and released Orchid and Janie looked up and realized that people were coming their way out of the darkness. She spotted Abby. Dorothy, Greyson, Colt, Daniel, the God Squad. When Janie saw Max, she released Orchid's hair and stepped back.

"What're you doing?" Greyson said—no, *yelled*—in a panic. He motioned toward the scissors. "What are you doing?"

Ethan glared at him.

"Stay out of it, you—" He added a word at the end. A slur that made Janie's heart stop.

Renni pointed at Orchid, who had rushed to Greyson and Dorothy.

"You're a liar!" Renni said. "You're nothing but poor white trash! You live with your dad in a work camp!" She looked at everyone else. "You think she's some big-city girl? Her mother's a junkie. Her mother's in *prison*. And she's been acting like some high-and-mighty princess, treating you like trash! *She's* the trash!"

If Renni expected them to join the rallying cry, she had badly miscalculated. There was silence. Greyson put an arm around Orchid, and the others closed ranks around them.

"There's something seriously wrong with you," Daniel said, narrowing his eyes at Renni.

"Me?" Renni said. "There's something wrong with *me*?"

"Yes," said Colt.

Renni gestured at Orchid, nearly frantic. "*She's* the liar! She's been lying this whole time! Orchid isn't even her real name! Do you know that? *She lies!* You think she's all that? She's nothing!"

Janie felt like she was floating above the scene, watching everything from a distance, and when she looked down, she saw herself, standing with Renni and Ethan on one side, and everyone else on the other.

I'm on the wrong side, she thought.

"The only piece of trash here is you," Greyson said.

And then Ethan told him to shut up and shot that word out of his mouth again. Everything happened fast after that. Daniel—*Daniel,* of all people, the class clown with the curly red hair—flew forward and swung a fist toward Ethan's face, but missed, then Ethan swung back and Colt came in—big, tall Colt—and that was all it took because Ethan got punched in the chin and fell on the grass, sprawled out and cursing, and that's when Greyson stepped up and raised his fist, but Daniel held him back, saying, "He's not worth the trouble, he's not worth the trouble."

Hallie and Daelyn and Baylee watched with wide, round eyes, and one of them took off back toward the dance, or maybe it was two of them, or maybe it was all of them, Janie couldn't tell, because she was still standing there holding the scissors and could still feel the sensation of Orchid's hair on her palm.

That had been the plan all along, to cut off all her hair, to make her think they would, anyway, to leave her in the grass, that was the plan Janie had agreed to, wasn't it, and now she was holding Renni's scissors and Dorothy was coming her way. But who cared? I mean, it was *Dorothy Doucet*. What was *Dorothy Doucet* going to do? But maybe this wasn't Dorothy Doucet because her face looked different. It looked angry. Rageful. And Janie could see all of it because Dorothy's hair flew back as she approached, and Janie realized she wasn't walking toward her; she was walking toward Renni. And Dorothy's fist was clenched and raised, but Janie couldn't comprehend or calculate what was happening, because this was *Dorothy Doucet*, and Dorothy Doucet would never punch anyone, would she? But no, that's not what she was doing at all, she wasn't using her fist to *hit* Renni, she was using it to hold something, and when Dorothy's hand flew forward, they all saw what it was, and it was a fistful of dirt, and the dirt hit Renni directly in the face, and even though it didn't make a sound, it *felt* like it did, it felt like a sound that bounced off every surface, burrowed into the oak tree, burrowed under the earth, flew into the sky, sailed through the crowds, drowned out the music, made everything quiet. Renni's eyes immediately blinked and watered and then she howled in anger and that was when Janie dropped the scissors.

A chaotic mass of voices swelled in their direction.

The God Squad had summoned the adults.

In seconds they were surrounded by people Janie didn't know or recognize, because they were in Saintlodge, after all, and she didn't know the people here. Someone took her arm and pulled her away and she heard, amidst all the chaos, a repeated question, again and again, asked by one person after another, "Are you okay?" "Are you okay?" "Are you okay?" but they weren't talking to her; it was the kids from Fawn Creek, all talking to Orchid, crowding around her, comforting her, and talking to Greyson, "Are you okay?" and telling Dorothy, "Don't worry, we'll tell them what happened, we'll stick up for you," and no one was speaking to Janie, who was being led by the elbow by a woman she didn't know, back to the community center, all alone.

SUNDAY

❀ *48* ❀

P_{*link.*}

The water barely stirred. The mosquitoes were out—the mosquitoes were always out—and the faint smell of bug spray filled the air. Greyson stood still, moving only his hand as it slowly, slowly turned the reel handle. Turn, turn. His father stood next to him, far enough but not too far, doing the same thing.

"Lots of commotion at that dance last night, huh?" Mr. Broussard said.

"Yeah. I guess."

"Your mom says there was some kinda fight."

"Yeah." Greyson said. A mosquito landed on his thumb, but quickly flew away.

"I'm supposed to tell you that throwing punches isn't the answer. That's what your mom wants me to say." He sighed and winked. "But sometimes a man's gotta stand up for himself, right?"

Greyson paused. "I didn't—" *I didn't throw a punch.* "I mean. Yeah."

Mr. Broussard nodded, peering out at the water as the sun bared down. There was movement just under the surface, but it was gone as quickly as it arrived.

"Dad," Greyson said. "Can I ask you something?"

"Certainly."

Turn, turn. "How come it does more harm than good to throw them back?"

Mr. Broussard looked at him, confused. "Huh?"

"The fish," Greyson said. "When I was little, I wanted to throw the fish back, but you said it did more harm than good."

"Oh. Right." Mr. Broussard went back to staring at the creek. "Well. When you get your hook in a fish, it injures them. You don't wanna toss it back in the water like that. They wouldn't be able to survive."

"Oh."

"I suppose if you catch it, you're stuck with it."

"Like with me," Greyson said, before he had a chance to think.

"How do you mean?"

Greyson didn't move. "You got me, and you're stuck with me. It's too late to throw me back now."

He had meant it as a joke, but it didn't sound like one. A look came over Mr. Broussard's face—an expression Greyson had never seen before. It seemed to last an eternity.

"I may not understand you, son, but one thing's for certain," Mr. Broussard said, his voice even and sure. "You're a keeper."

Turn, turn.

"Besides," Mr. Broussard continued. "If I'm stuck with you, that only means one thing."

Greyson swallowed. "What?"

"It means you're stuck with me, too." He squinted into the sun. "You can't choose your family."

Greyson thought of standing together with Orchid and Didi in the kitchen, walking home from school, entering the dance, arms linked.

I'm not sure about that, he thought.

When Didi got home from the dance, her parents told her to sit down. She chose the striped armchair. Her parents sat on the couch across from her.

"You harmed another girl," Mrs. Doucet said. The word

"harmed" felt strange and old-fashioned, just like the room they were in. "I don't understand this behavior. It's like it fell out of the clear blue sky."

Didi imagined herself falling from the clouds, hair flying around her face, arms outstretched like wings.

"Why'd you do it?" her father asked.

The question caught Didi off guard. She couldn't remember the last time her father had asked her a question.

"Renni deserved it," said Didi. Her voice sounded more forceful than she expected.

"There are better ways to handle things," Mrs. Doucet said, though she didn't explain what those ways were. Instead, she opened her hand and thrust it in the space between them. "Give me your phone. You'll get it back in one week. And we'll talk more about this later."

Didi didn't argue. She dutifully surrendered her phone, then stood up and walked toward her room without another word. Her mother's voice trailed behind her.

"Dorothy Claire Doucet," she said, like it was a complete sentence. Didi paused without turning around. "You really surprised me tonight."

Didi continued down the hall, not bothering to hide her smile. When she climbed into bed, she was convinced that she would never be able to fall asleep—her whole body buzzed with adrenaline—but she drifted off quickly, like she hadn't slept in years. She didn't open her eyes until she felt the warmth of the mid-morning sun. The first thing she did was reach for her phone before remembering she didn't have it.

The dance replayed in her mind. Every second, every moment. When the replay ended, she played it again. She was desperate to talk to Greyson or Orchid. She was desperate to check her phone, to see if Colt had texted her. It was possible, right?

When she tired of replaying the night, she changed things up. Created different scenarios. In one of them, she and Colt slow danced without even blushing. In another, she told Renni off before slapping her in the face. In another, Orchid never went outside at all and instead the three of them hit the dance floor and—to quote one of Mrs. Broussard's pillows—*dance like no one's watching*. There were a million possibilities, but one constant stayed true in all of them. Dorothy Doucet—Didi—was never in the background. She was front and center, surprising everyone.

"Mom says you can't be friends with Renni anymore. Is that true?"

Janie opened her eyes. Mee-Wee was there, at her bedside, fully awake, fully dressed, holding a blue Blow

Pop. Her entire mouth, including her tongue, was blue. The air smelled like cotton candy.

"What time is it?" Janie mumbled.

"It's almost noon." Mee-Wee shoved the Blow Pop into her mouth. She talked around it, garbling her voice. "She sahd you hafta get up and help at the restahrant."

"Ugh," Janie said. She threw the comforter over her head.

Mee-Wee tapped her through the blanket. "So, is it true?"

"Is what true?"

"That you can't be friends with Renni anymore."

"Yes." Ugh. She did *not* want to go to the restaurant today. She didn't want to go anywhere. She wanted to stay right here, in bed, for the rest of her life.

"Are you sad about it?"

"I have other things on my mind, Mee-Wee."

"Like what?"

"Like *things*." Janie lightly kicked her foot in Mee-Wee's direction. "Now get out. Tell Mom I'm awake."

"Fine," Mee-Wee said. Her footsteps faded away. The door clicked closed, but Janie stayed where she was, under the covers.

She didn't have other things on her mind, really. She only had one thing—Orchid.

How would she face her at school on Monday? What would she, Janie, say? What would Orchid say? What would the other kids think?

All Janie knew for certain was that a tight ball of regret and guilt had collected in the pit of her belly and she didn't know how to make it go away. Maybe if she just *talked* to Orchid, got her to *understand*, everything would be better.

But understand what?

We didn't mean anything by it, Orchid. We just wanted to cut off all your hair then leave you in the grass. But wait—no, no, no, we weren't really going to cut it, see. Renni just wanted you to think we were. Yeah, I know it seemed like we were really going to do it, but it was all for show. You understand, right? We just wanted to teach you a lesson. We found out you were a liar. You can't just go around making stuff up, just because you think you're better than us. That's why you did it, right? Because you think you're better than us?

I wasn't going to do it, Orchid.

I was going to save you.

I promise. I was.

MONDAY

49

Greyson had never been sent to the principal's office before, but here he was. He'd been desperate to get inside Mr. Agosto's classroom to see Orchid and Didi—neither of whom he'd spoken to since the dance—but he didn't even have a chance to sit down before Mr. Agosto told him he needed to go see Principal Abrams.

The principal's office was sterile and clean, with two uncomfortable-looking chairs across from a big desk. Greyson sat in one of them. Principal Abrams wasn't there yet, but Greyson was assured that he was on his way.

One of his mother's pillows was perched on the chair next to him. Mrs. Broussard's pillows were everywhere in

Fawn Creek. You couldn't escape them. This one said *Make your life a masterpiece.*

Greyson pressed his fingertips together. They ached from all the work he'd done with his mother over the weekend, learning how to operate the sewing machine, learning how to hem pants, learning about threads and fabrics.

"I wish I'd taught you all this earlier," his mother said Sunday afternoon. "You're good at it. I could've gotten much more work done."

"It's not really a boy thing, I guess," Greyson said.

His mother paused. Smiled. "It's an anyone thing. Better yet—it's a *Greyson* thing."

Yes.

Yes, it was.

Greyson was desperate to talk to Didi. He wanted to know what it felt like to throw dirt in Renni Dean's face while everyone watched. He wanted to see how the kids at school would react to her. What would they say? What would *she* say?

He was desperate to talk to Orchid, too.

He wanted to know if she was okay. If she needed anything.

He wanted her to know that they were all on her side.

His knee bounced. Why was he in the principal's

office, anyway? He hadn't done anything wrong. He needed to be in Mr. Agosto's class. He needed to check on his friends.

Principal Abrams's voice boomed from behind him. "Good morning, Greyson."

Greyson turned and watched the man stride to his chair.

"Good morning, Principal Abrams," he said.

Abrams glanced at Greyson's outfit quizzically. Greyson had almost forgotten what he was wearing—a bright pink T-shirt with the words "Exist Loudly" painted in black and a pair of oversized jeans with one of his mother's scarves as a belt.

"What are you wearing?" Trevor had said that morning as he slipped on his backpack.

"These are called clothes," Greyson said.

Trevor snorted. "You look like a freak."

"Thank you," Greyson said.

When it was time to get into his father's truck for a ride to school, Greyson politely declined.

"I'll walk," he said. He was halfway out the door when he heard the grumbling voice of his father—too low for Greyson to hear what he was saying. But he heard his mother clearly.

"Greyson is free to wear whatever he wants, just like

Trevor or anyone else," she said. "There's nothing wrong with—"

Greyson didn't listen to the rest; he didn't want to, didn't need to. He smiled and walked into the morning sun, feeling lighter than a feather, despite all the snickers as he sauntered down the sidewalk, as he went up the stairs, as he made his way down the hall. Greyson imagined that each laugh, each stare, each snicker was a cookie, and he ate and ate and ate until he was full and happy.

He took Principal Abrams's glare and ate that, too.

He straightened. Sat tall.

"I wanted to talk to you about the conduct of the Fawn Creek students at the dance in Saintlodge on Friday," Principal Abrams said. He leaned forward on his meaty arms. "I want to make sure each one of you remembers that when you step off this property, you are still a representative of your community. Wherever you go, whatever you do, you represent Fawn Creek. You—all of you—need to understand that when you do something, good or bad, people will look at you, and your behavior, and they'll think 'that's one of those kids from Fawn Creek' . . ."

Principal Abrams's mouth kept moving, but the words disappeared into the air.

Not me, Greyson thought. *That's not what people will*

think of me. Not forever. I may be a kid from Fawn Creek, but that's not all I am. And besides . . .

Besides.

On Friday night the kids from Fawn Creek—everyone but Janie, that is—had been on the right side.

Maybe they didn't do everything exactly as they should have.

Maybe Didi didn't need to hit Renni in the face with dirt.

Maybe Greyson didn't need to raise his fist at Ethan when he called him that name.

Maybe this, maybe that.

But Greyson wasn't ashamed. He was proud.

The other kids from Fawn Creek had gathered around him to make sure he was okay. They had stood up for him. When Ethan came forward, so did they. And they didn't have to. He didn't ask them to. He didn't even *expect* them to.

But they did.

In the chaos afterward, they promised Didi they'd look out for her.

And they did.

They took care of Orchid, too.

"Mr. Abrams—" Greyson said, though the principal was still talking. "Have you talked to Orchid already? Is she okay?"

Greyson had wanted to visit her over the weekend, but his mother told him to leave it alone, give it a few days. A few days for what? He didn't know.

Principal Abrams sighed, as if Greyson's impolite interruption only proved his point. "I was *speaking*, Mr. Broussard."

"I know. I'm sorry," Greyson said.

"But to answer your question . . . no." Mr. Abrams leaned back. The chair groaned. "Orchid, as you call her, has already transferred out."

Greyson's stomach dropped.

"Transferred out?" he said.

"That's what I said."

"Because of what happened? Because of Friday?"

"No," Mr. Abrams said. "Because her father finished up last week. Saturday was his last day on the job."

Orchid was gone.

She left and didn't tell them.

Why?

There was no way to ask. No way to know.

What was she thinking? Where was she going? Where was she, right now?

She could be anywhere.

"You may go, Mr. Broussard," Mr. Abrams said.

Greyson didn't move at first. But then he managed it. He

put both feet on the ground. He stood up. He walked out. He wanted to bolt, run down the hall, barge into Mr. Agosto's room, tell Didi—tell all of them—*She's gone! She's gone!* But as soon as he stepped out of Mr. Abrams's office, he was face-to-face with Janie, who was on her way in.

Janie looked tired.

Janie looked sad.

Janie said, "Hi."

Greyson wasn't going to say anything at first. But he said, "Hi."

She paused. "I'm sorry," she said. Her voice shook. Her eyes watered. Was she going to cry? In all the years they'd grown up together, he had never seen Janie Crawford cry. But yes, she was crying. "Will you tell her for me? Tell her I'm sorry?"

Greyson didn't know what to say.

How could he tell Orchid that Janie was sorry?

"If I see her," he said, "I'll tell her."

It was the best he could do.

Didi looked up and smiled when he came in.

He glanced at Orchid's empty desk as he sat down. The students' I Am poems were tacked along the wall. They should all take an opportunity to read them, Mr. Agosto was saying. But Greyson didn't hear. Didn't care.

He turned around and looked at Didi. He could see her eyes clearly because she had her hair back, off her shoulders, away from her face.

"She's gone," he whispered.

"I know," Didi said. "But we're still here."

"For now," Greyson said.

"Yes," Didi replied. "For now."

I AM

"I Am"

By Orchid Mason

I am imaginative and kind.
I wonder what the ocean looks like.
I hear the call of faraway birds.
I see another place I want to be.
I want to go there.
I am imaginative and kind.

I pretend I live a different life.
I feel that I could be someone else.
I touch the flower in my hair.
I worry I will always be me.
I cry when I feel lonely.
I am imaginative and kind.

I understand that I am me.
I say, "I want to live a different life."
I dream that I will someday.
I try to remember that someday is just around the corner.
I hope that's true.
I am imaginative and kind.

ERIN ENTRADA KELLY was awarded the Newbery Medal for *Hello, Universe* and a Newbery Honor for *We Dream of Space*. She grew up in Lake Charles, Louisiana, and now lives in Delaware. She is a professor of children's literature in the graduate fiction and publishing programs at Rosemont College, where she earned her MFA, and is on the faculty at Hamline University. Her short fiction has been nominated for the Philippines Free Press Literary Award for Short Fiction and the Pushcart Prize. Before becoming a children's author, Erin worked as a journalist and magazine editor and received numerous awards for community service journalism, feature writing, and editing from the Louisiana Press Association and the Associated Press.

Erin Entrada Kelly's debut novel, *Blackbird Fly*, was a Kirkus Best Book, a School Library Journal Best Book, an ALSC Notable Book, and an Asian/Pacific American Literature Honor Book. She is also the author of *The Land of Forgotten Girls*, winner of the Asian/Pacific American Award for Literature; *You Go First*, a Spring 2018 Indie Next Pick; *Lalani of the Distant Sea*, an Indie Next Pick; and two novels for younger readers, *Maybe Maybe Marisol Rainey* and *Surely Surely Marisol Rainey*, which she also illustrated.